133 is a agab

2

ROOTABAGA STORIES

BY

CARL SANDBURG

ILLUSTRATIONS AND DECORATIONS
BY
MAUD AND MISKA PETERSHAM

NEW YORK
HARCOURT, BRACE AND COMPANY

CONTENTS

Part One: Rootabaga Stories

1.

Three Stories About the Finding of the Zigzag Railroad, the Pigs with Bibs On, the Circus Clown Ovens, the Village of Liver-and-Onions, the Village of Cream Puffs

How They Broke Away to Go to the Rootabaga Country   *3*

How They Bring Back the Village of Cream Puffs When the Wind Blows It Away   *19*

How the Five Rusty Rats Helped Find a New Village   *29*

2.

Five Stories About the Potato Face Blind Man

The Potato Face Blind Man Who Lost the Diamond Rabbit on His Gold Accordion   *41*

How the Potato Face Blind Man Enjoyed Himself on a Fine Spring Morning   *45*

Poker Face the Baboon and Hot Dog the Tiger   *53*

The Toboggan-to-the-Moon Dream of the Potato Face Blind Man   *59*

How Gimme the Ax Found Out About the Zigzag Railroad and Who Made It Zigzag   *65*

3.

Three Stories About the Gold Buckskin Whincher

The Story of Blixie Bimber and the Power of the Gold Buckskin Whincher   *73*

Contents

The Story of Jason Squiff and Why He Had a Popcorn Hat, Popcorn Mittens and Popcorn Shoes 79

The Story of Rags Habakuk, the Two Blue Rats, and the Circus Man Who Came With Spot Cash Money 89

4.

Four Stories About the Deep Doom of Dark Doorways

The Wedding Procession of the Rag Doll and the Broom Handle and Who Was in It 99

How the Hat Ashes Shovel Helped Snoo Foo 105

Three Boys with Jugs of Molasses and Secret Ambitions 109

How Bimbo the Snip's Thumb Stuck to His Nose When the Wind Changed 123

5.

Three Stories About Three Ways the Wind Went Winding

The Two Skyscrapers Who Decided to Have a Child 133

The Dollar Watch and the Five Jack Rabbits 141

The Wooden Indian and the Shaghorn Buffalo 151

6.

Four Stories About Dear, Dear Eyes

The White Horse Girl and the Blue Wind Boy 159

What Six Girls with Balloons Told the Gray Man on Horseback 167

How Henry Hagglyhoagly Played the Guitar With His Mittens On 175

Never Kick a Slipper at the Moon 185

Contents

7.

One Story—"Only the Fire-Born Understand Blue"

Sand Flat Shadows   *191*

8.

Two Stories About Corn Fairies, Blue Foxes, Flong-boos and Happenings that Happened in the United States and Canada

How to Tell Corn Fairies When You See 'Em   *205*
How the Animals Lost Their Tails and Got Them Back Traveling from Philadelphia to Medicine Hat   *213*

Part Two: Rootabaga Pigeons

1.

Two Stories Told by the Potato Face Blind Man

The Skyscraper to the Moon and How the Green Rat with the Rheumatism Ran a Thousand Miles Twice   *3*
Slipfoot and How He Nearly Always Never Gets What He Goes After   *9*

2.

Two Stories About Bugs and Eggs

Many, Many Weddings in One Corner House   *19*
Shush Shush, the Big Buff Banty Hen Who Laid an Egg in the Postmaster's Hat   *27*

Contents

3.

Five Stories About Hatrack the Horse, Six Pigeons, Three Wild Babylonian Baboons, Six Umbrellas, Bozo the Button Buster

How Ragbag Mammy Kept Her Secret While the Wind Blew Away the Village of Hat Pins   *33*

How Six Pigeons Came Back to Hatrack the Horse After Many Accidents and Six Telegrams   *41*

How the Three Wild Babylonian Baboons Went Away in the Rain Eating Bread and Butter   *49*

How Six Umbrellas Took Off Their Straw Hats to Show Respect to the One Big Umbrella   *55*

How Bozo the Button Buster Busted All His Buttons When a Mouse Came   *63*

4.

Two Stories About Four Boys Who Had Different Dreams

How Googler and Gaggler, the Two Christmas Babies, Came Home with Monkey Wrenches   *75*

How Johnny the Wham Sleeps in Money All the Time and Joe the Wimp Shines and Sees Things   *87*

5.

Two Stories Told by the Potato Face Blind Man About Two Girls with Red Hearts

How Deep Red Roses Goes Back and Forth Between the Clock and the Looking Glass   *97*

How Pink Peony Sent Spuds, the Ballplayer, Up to Pick Four Moons   *105*

Contents

6.

Three Stories About Moonlight, Pigeons, Bees, Egypt, Jesse James, Spanish Onions, the Queen of the Cracked Heads, the King of the Paper Sacks

How Dippy the Wisp and Slip Me Liz Came in the Moonshine Where the Potato Face Blind Man Sat with His Accordion *115*

How Hot Balloons and His Pigeon Daughters Crossed Over into the Rootabaga Country *127*

How Two Sweetheart Dippies Sat in the Moonlight on a Lumber Yard Fence and Heard About the Sooners and the Boomers *139*

7.

Two Stories Out of the Tall Grass

The Haystack Cricket and How Things Are Different Up in the Moon Towns *153*

Why the Big Ball Game Between Hot Grounders and the Grand Standers Was a Hot Game *161*

8.

Two Stories Out of Oklahoma and Nebraska

The Huckabuck Family and How They Raised Pop Corn in Nebraska and Quit and Came Back *169*

Yang Yang and Hoo Hoo, or the Song of the Left Foot of the Shadow of the Goose *181*

Contents

9.

One Story About Big People Now and Little People
Long Ago

How a Skyscraper and a Railroad Train Got Picked Up and
Carried Away from Pig's Eye Valley Far in the Pickax
Mountains *191*

10.

Three Stories About the Letter X and How It Got
into the Alphabet

Pig Wisps *201*
Kiss Me *207*
Blue Silver *215*

FULL-PAGE ILLUSTRATIONS

Part One: Rootabaga Stories

PAGE

He opened the ragbag and took out all the spot cash money 7

Then the uncles asked her the first question first . 21

They held on to the long curved tails of the rusty rats 33

"I am sure many people will stop and remember the Potato Face Blind Man" 47

His hat was popcorn, his mittens popcorn and his shoes popcorn 83

They stepped into the molasses with their bare feet . 113

The monkey took the place of the traffic policeman . 129

So they stood looking 153

It seemed to him as though the sky came down close to his nose 177

Away off where the sun was coming up there were people and animals 195

There on a high stool in a high tower on a high hill sits the Head Spotter of the Weather Makers . 215

ix

Full-Page Illustrations

Part Two: Rootabaga Pigeons

PAGE

On the last step of the stairway my foot slips . . 11

The Hot Cookie Pan came with a pan of hot cookies
and the Coal Bucket with coal 21

The mouse bit the knot and cut it loose . . . 67

They went to sleep on top of the wagon . . . 81

She was sitting on a ladder feeding baby clocks to
the baby alligators 119

One of the pigeons rang the bell 129

She carried the squash into the kitchen . . . 171

Out into the snowstorm Flax Eyes rode that day . 209

ROOTABAGA STORIES

TO
SPINK AND SKABOOTCH

1. Three Stories About the Finding of the Zigzag Railroad, the Pigs with Bibs On, the Circus Clown Ovens, the Village of Liver-and-Onions, the Village of Cream Puffs.

People: Gimme the Ax

Please Gimme

Ax Me No Questions

The Ticket Agent

Wing Tip the Spick

The Four Uncles

The Rat in a Blizzard

The Five Rusty Rats

More People:

Balloon Pickers

Baked Clowns

Polka Dot Pigs

How They Broke Away to Go to the
Rootabaga Country

Gimme the Ax lived in a house where everything is the same as it always was.

"The chimney sits on top of the house and lets the smoke out," said Gimme the Ax. "The doorknobs open the doors. The windows are always either open or shut. We are always either upstairs or downstairs in this house. Everything is the same as it always was."

So he decided to let his children name themselves.

3

"The first words they speak as soon as they learn to make words shall be their names," he said. "They shall name themselves."

When the first boy came to the house of Gimme the Ax, he was named Please Gimme. When the first girl came she was named Ax Me No Questions.

And both of the children had the shadows of valleys by night in their eyes and the lights of early morning, when the sun is coming up, on their foreheads.

And the hair on top of their heads was a dark wild grass. And they loved to turn the doorknobs, open the doors, and run out to have the wind comb their hair and touch their eyes and put its six soft fingers on their foreheads.

And then because no more boys came and no more girls came, Gimme the Ax said to himself, "My first boy is my last and my last girl is my first and they picked their names themselves."

Please Gimme grew up and his ears got longer. Ax Me No Questions grew up and her ears got longer. And they kept on living in the house where everything is the same as it always was. They learned to say just as their father said, "The chimney sits on top of the house and lets the smoke out, the doorknobs open the doors, the windows are always either open or shut, we are always either upstairs or downstairs—everything is the same as it always was."

After a while they began asking each other in the cool of the evening after they had eggs for breakfast in the morning, "Who's who? How much? And what's the answer?"

"It is too much to be too long anywhere," said the tough old man, Gimme the Ax.

And Please Gimme and Ax Me No Questions, the tough son and the tough daughter of Gimme the Ax, answered their father, "It *is* too much to be too long anywhere."

So they sold everything they had, pigs, pastures, pepper pickers, pitchforks, everything except their ragbags and a few extras.

When their neighbors saw them selling everything they had, the different neighbors said, "They are going to Kansas, to Kokomo, to Canada, to Kankakee, to Kalamazoo, to Kamchatka, to the Chattahoochee."

One little sniffer with his eyes half shut and a mitten on his nose, laughed in his hat five ways and said, "They are going to the moon and when they get there they will find everything is the same as it always was."

All the spot cash money he got for selling everything, pigs, pastures, pepper pickers, pitchforks, Gimme the Ax put in a ragbag and slung on his back like a rag picker going home.

Then he took Please Gimme, his oldest and youngest and only son, and Ax Me No Questions, his oldest and youngest and only daughter, and went to the railroad station.

The ticket agent was sitting at the window selling railroad tickets the same as always.

He opened the ragbag and took out all the
spot cash money

"Do you wish a ticket to go away and come back or do you wish a ticket to go away and *never* come back?" the ticket agent asked wiping sleep out of his eyes.

"We wish a ticket to ride where the railroad tracks run off into the sky and never come back—send us far as the railroad rails go and then forty ways farther yet," was the reply of Gimme the Ax.

"So far? So early? So soon?" asked the ticket agent wiping more sleep out his eyes. "Then I will give you a new ticket. It blew in. It is a long slick yellow leather slab ticket with a blue spanch across it."

Gimme the Ax thanked the ticket agent once, thanked the ticket agent twice, and then instead of thanking the ticket agent three times he opened the ragbag and took out all the spot cash money he got for selling everything, pigs, pastures, pepper pickers, pitchforks, and paid the spot cash money to the ticket agent.

Before he put it in his pocket he looked once,

twice, three times at the long yellow leather slab ticket with a blue spanch across it.

Then with Please Gimme and Ax Me No Questions he got on the railroad train, showed the conductor his ticket and they started to ride to where the railroad tracks run off into the blue sky and then forty ways farther yet.

The train ran on and on. It came to the place where the railroad tracks run off into the blue sky. And it ran on and on chick chick-a-chick chick-a-chick chick-a-chick.

Sometimes the engineer hooted and tooted the whistle. Sometimes the fireman rang the bell. Sometimes the open-and-shut of the steam hog's nose choked and spit pfisty-pfoost, pfisty-pfoost, pfisty-pfoost. But no matter what happened to the whistle and the bell and the steam hog, the train ran on and on to where the railroad tracks run off into the blue sky. And then it ran on and on more and more.

Sometimes Gimme the Ax looked in his pocket, put his fingers in and took out the long slick yellow leather slab ticket with a blue spanch across it.

"Not even the Kings of Egypt with all their climbing camels, and all their speedy, spotted, lucky lizards, ever had a ride like this," he said to his children.

Then something happened. They met another train running on the same track. One train was going one way. The other was going the other way. They met. They passed each other.

"What was it—what happened?" the children asked their father.

"One train went over, the other train went under," he answered. "This is the Over and Under country. Nobody gets out of the way of anybody else. They either go over or under."

Next they came to the country of the balloon pickers. Hanging down from the sky strung on strings so fine the eye could not see them at first, was the balloon crop of that summer. The sky was thick with balloons. Red, blue, yellow balloons, white, purple and orange balloons—peach, watermelon and potato balloons—rye loaf and wheat loaf balloons—link sausage and pork chop balloons—they floated and filled the sky.

The balloon pickers were walking on high stilts picking balloons. Each picker had his own stilts, long or short. For picking balloons near the ground he had short stilts. If he wanted to pick far and high he walked on a far and high pair of stilts.

Baby pickers on baby stilts were picking baby balloons. When they fell off the stilts the handful of balloons they were holding kept them in the air till they got their feet into the stilts again.

"Who is that away up there in the sky climbing like a bird in the morning?" Ax Me No Questions asked her father.

"He was singing too happy," replied the father. "The songs came out of his neck and made him so light the balloons pulled him off his stilts."

"Will he ever come down again back to his own people?"

"Yes, his heart will get heavy when his songs are all gone. Then he will drop down to his stilts again."

The train was running on and on. The engineer hooted and tooted the whistle when he felt like it. The fireman rang the bell when he felt that way. And sometimes the open-and-shut of the steam hog had to go pfisty-pfoost, pfisty-pfoost.

"Next is the country where the circus clowns come from," said Gimme the Ax to his son and daughter. "Keep your eyes open."

They did keep their eyes open. They saw cities with ovens, long and short ovens, fat stubby ovens, lean lank ovens, all for baking either long or short clowns, or fat and stubby or lean and lank clowns.

After each clown was baked in the oven it

was taken out into the sunshine and put up to stand like a big white doll with a red mouth leaning against the fence.

Two men came along to each baked clown standing still like a doll. One man threw a bucket of white fire over it. The second man pumped a wind pump with a living red wind through the red mouth.

The clown rubbed his eyes, opened his mouth, twisted his neck, wiggled his ears, wriggled his toes, jumped away from the fence and began turning handsprings, cartwheels, somersaults and flipflops in the sawdust ring near the fence.

"The next we come to is the Rootabaga Country where the big city is the Village of Liver-and-Onions," said Gimme the Ax, looking again in his pocket to be sure he had the long slick yellow leather slab ticket with a blue spanch across it.

The train ran on and on till it stopped running straight and began running in zigzags like one letter Z put next to another Z and the next and the next.

The tracks and the rails and the ties and the spikes under the train all stopped being straight and changed to zigzags like one letter Z and another letter Z put next after the other.

"It seems like we go half way and then back up," said Ax Me No Questions.

"Look out of the window and see if the pigs have bibs on," said Gimme the Ax. "If the pigs are wearing bibs then this is the Rootabaga country."

And they looked out of the zigzagging windows of the zigzagging cars and the first pigs they saw had bibs on. And the next pigs and the next pigs they saw all had bibs on.

The checker pigs had checker bibs on, the striped pigs had striped bibs on. And the polka dot pigs had polka dot bibs on.

"Who fixes it for the pigs to have bibs on?" Please Gimme asked his father.

"The fathers and mothers fix it," answered

Gimme the Ax. "The checker pigs have checker fathers and mothers. The striped pigs have striped fathers and mothers. And the polka dot pigs have polka dot fathers and mothers."

And the train went zigzagging on and on running on the tracks and the rails and the spikes and the ties which were all zigzag like the letter Z and the letter Z.

And after a while the train zigzagged on into the Village of Liver-and-Onions, known as the biggest city in the big, big Rootabaga country.

And so if you are going to the Rootabaga country you will know when you get there because the railroad tracks change from straight to zigzag, the pigs have bibs on and it is the fathers and mothers who fix it.

And if you start to go to that country remember first you must sell everything you have, pigs, pastures, pepper pickers, pitchforks, put the spot cash money in a ragbag and go to the railroad station and ask the ticket agent for a long slick yellow leather slab ticket with a blue spanch across it.

And you mustn't be surprised if the ticket agent wipes sleep from his eyes and asks, "So far?   So early?   So soon?"

How They Bring Back the Village of Cream Puffs When the Wind Blows It Away

A girl named Wing Tip the Spick came to the Village of Liver-and-Onions to visit her uncle and her uncle's uncle on her mother's side and her uncle and her uncle's uncle on her father's side.

It was the first time the four uncles had a chance to see their little relation, their niece. Each one of the four uncles was proud of the blue eyes of Wing Tip the Spick.

19

How They Bring Back Village

The two uncles on her mother's side took a long deep look into her blue eyes and said, "Her eyes are so blue, such a clear light blue, they are the same as cornflowers with blue raindrops shining and dancing on silver leaves after a sun shower in any of the summer months."

And the two uncles on her father's side, after taking a long deep look into the eyes of Wing Tip the Spick, said, "Her eyes are so blue, such a clear light shining blue, they are the same as cornflowers with blue raindrops shining and dancing on the silver leaves after a sun shower in any of the summer months."

And though Wing Tip the Spick didn't listen and didn't hear what the uncles said about her blue eyes, she did say to herself when they were not listening, "I know these are sweet uncles and I am going to have a sweet time visiting my relations."

The four uncles said to her, "Will you let us ask you two questions, first the first question and second the second question?"

Then the uncles asked her the first question first

"I will let you ask me fifty questions this morning, fifty questions tomorrow morning, and fifty questions any morning. I like to listen to questions. They slip in one ear and slip out of the other."

Then the uncles asked her the first question first, "Where do you come from?" and the second question second, "Why do you have two freckles on your chin?"

"Answering your first question first," said Wing Tip the Spick, "I come from the Village of Cream Puffs, a little light village on the upland corn prairie. From a long ways off it looks like a little hat you could wear on the end of your thumb to keep the rain off your thumb."

"Tell us more," said one uncle. "Tell us much," said another uncle. "Tell it without stopping," added another uncle. "Interruptions nix nix," murmured the last of the uncles.

"It is a light little village on the upland corn prairie many miles past the sunset in the west," went on Wing Tip the Spick. "It is light the same as a cream puff is light. It sits all by itself on the big long prairie where the prairie goes up in a slope. There on the slope the winds play around the village. They sing it wind songs, summer wind songs in summer, winter wind songs in winter."

"And sometimes like an accident, the wind gets rough. And when the wind gets rough it picks up the little Village of Cream Puffs and blows it away off in the sky—all by itself."

"O-o-h-h," said one uncle. "Um-m-m-m," said the other three uncles.

"Now the people in the village all understand the winds with their wind songs in summer and winter. And they understand the rough wind who comes sometimes and picks up the village and blows it away off high in the sky all by itself.

"If you go to the public square in the middle of the village you will see a big roundhouse. If you take the top off the roundhouse you will see a big spool with a long string winding up around the spool.

"Now whenever the rough wind comes and picks up the village and blows it away off high in the sky all by itself then the string winds loose off the spool, because the village is fastened to the string. So the rough wind blows and blows and the string on the spool winds looser and looser the farther the village goes blowing away off into the sky all by itself.

"Then at last when the rough wind, so forgetful, so careless, has had all the fun it wants, then the people of the village all come together and begin to wind up the spool and bring back the village where it was before."

"O-o-h-h," said one uncle. "Um-m-m-m," said the other three uncles.

"And sometimes when you come to the village to see your little relation, your niece who has four such sweet uncles, maybe she will lead you through the middle of the city to the public square and show you the roundhouse. They call it the Roundhouse of the Big Spool. And they are proud because it was thought up and is there to show when visitors come."

"And now will you answer the second question second—why do you have two freckles on your chin?" interrupted the uncle who had said before, "Interruptions nix nix."

"The freckles are put on," answered Wing Tip the Spick. "When a girl goes away from the Village of Cream Puffs her mother puts on two freckles, on the chin. Each freckle must be the same as a little burnt cream puff kept in the oven too long. After the two freckles looking like two little burnt cream puffs are put on her chin, they remind the girl every morning when she combs her hair and looks in the looking glass. They remind her where she came from and she mustn't stay away too long."

"O-h-h-h," said one uncle. "Um-m-m-m," said the other three uncles. And they talked among each other afterward, the four uncles by themselves, saying:

26

"She has a gift. It is her eyes. They are so blue, such a clear light blue, the same as corn-flowers with blue raindrops shining and dancing on silver leaves after a sun shower in any of the summer months."

At the same time Wing Tip the Spick was saying to herself, "I know for sure now these are sweet uncles and I am going to have a sweet time visiting my relations."

How the Five Rusty Rats Helped Find a New Village

One day while Wing Tip the Spick was visiting her four uncles in the Village of Liver-and-Onions, a blizzard came up. Snow filled the sky and the wind blew and made a noise like heavy wagon axles grinding and crying.

And on this day a gray rat came to the house of the four uncles, a rat with gray skin and gray hair, gray as the gray gravy on a beefsteak. The rat had a basket. In the basket was a catfish. And the rat said, "Please let me have a little fire and a little salt as I wish to make a little bowl of hot catfish soup to keep me warm through the blizzard."

And the four uncles all said together, "This is no time for rats to be around—and we would like to ask you where you got the catfish in the basket."

"Oh, oh, oh, please—in the name of the five rusty rats, the five lucky rats of the Village of Cream Puffs, please don't," was the exclamation of Wing Tip the Spick.

The uncles stopped. They looked long and deep into the eyes of Wing Tip the Spick and thought, as they had thought before, how her eyes were clear light blue the same as cornflowers with blue raindrops shining on the silver leaves in a summer sun shower.

And the four uncles opened the door and let the gray rat come in with the basket and the catfish. They showed the gray rat the way to the kitchen and the fire and the salt. And they watched the rat and kept him company while he fixed himself a catfish soup to keep him warm traveling through the blizzard with the sky full of snow.

After they opened the front door and let the rat out and said good-by, they turned to Wing Tip the Spick and asked her to tell them about the five rusty lucky rats of the Village of Cream Puffs where she lived with her father and her mother and her folks.

"When I was a little girl growing up, before I learned all I learned since I got older, my grandfather gave me a birthday present because I was nine years old. I remember how he said to me, 'You will never be nine years old again after this birthday, so I give you this box for a birthday present.'

"In the box was a pair of red slippers with a gold clock on each slipper. One of the clocks ran fast. The other clock ran slow. And he told me if I wished to be early anywhere I should go by the clock that ran fast. And if I wished to be late anywhere I should go by the clock that ran slow.

31

"And that same birthday he took me down through the middle of the Village of Cream Puffs to the public square near the Roundhouse of the Big Spool. There he pointed his finger at the statue of the five rusty rats, the five lucky rats. And as near as I can remember his words, he said:

" 'Many years ago, long before the snow birds began to wear funny little slip-on hats and funny little slip-on shoes, and away back long before the snow birds learned how to slip off their slip-on hats and how to slip off their slip-on shoes, long ago in the faraway Village of Liver-and-Onions, the people who ate cream puffs came together and met in the streets and picked up their baggage and put their belongings on their shoulders and marched out of the Village of Liver-and-Onions saying, "We shall find a new place for a village and the name of it shall be the Village of Cream Puffs.

" 'They marched out on the prairie with their baggage and belongings in sacks on their

32

They held on to the long curved tails of
the rusty rats

shoulders. And a blizzard came up. Snow filled the sky. The wind blew and blew and made a noise like heavy wagon axles grinding and crying.

" 'The snow came on. The wind twisted all day and all night and all the next day. The wind changed black and twisted and spit icicles in their faces. They got lost in the blizzard. They expected to die and be buried in the snow for the wolves to come and eat them.

" 'Then the five lucky rats came, the five rusty rats, rust on their skin and hair, rust on their feet and noses, rust all over, and especially, most especially of all, rust on their long curved tails. They dug their noses down into the snow and their long curved tails stuck up far above the snow where the people who were lost in the blizzard could take hold of the tails like handles.

" 'And so, while the wind and the snow blew and the blizzard beat its icicles in their faces, they held on to the long curved tails of the rusty rats till they came to the place where the Village of Cream Puffs now stands. It was the rusty rats who saved their lives and showed them where to put their new village. That is why this statue now stands in the public square, this statue of the shapes of the five rusty rats, the five lucky rats with their noses down in the snow and their long curved tails lifted high out of the snow.'

"That is the story as my grandfather told it to me. And he said it happened long ago, long before the snow birds began to wear slip-on hats and slip-on shoes, long before they learned how to slip off the slip-on hats and to slip off the slip-on shoes."

"O-h-h-h," said one of the uncles. "Um-m-m-m," said the other three uncles.

"And sometime," added Wing Tip the Spick, "when you go away from the Village of Liver-and-Onions and cross the Shampoo River and ride many miles across the upland prairie till you come to the Village of Cream Puffs, you will find a girl there who loves four uncles very much.

"And if you ask her politely, she will show you the red slippers with gold clocks on them, one clock to be early by, the other to be late by. And if you are still more polite she will take you through the middle of the town to the public square and show you the statue of the five rusty lucky rats with their long curved tails sticking up in the air like handles. And the tails are curved so long and so nice you will feel like going up and taking hold of them to see what will happen to you."

2. Five Stories About the Potato Face Blind Man

People: The Potato Face Blind Man
Any Ice Today
Pick Ups
Lizzie Lazarus
Poker Face the Baboon
Hot Dog the Tiger
Whitson Whimble
A Man Shoveling Money
A Watermelon Moon
White Gold Boys
Blue Silver Girls
Big White Moon Spiders
Zizzies
Gimme the Ax Again

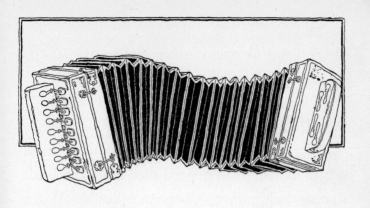

The Potato Face Blind Man Who Lost the Diamond Rabbit on His Gold Accordion

There was a Potato Face Blind Man used to play an accordion on the Main Street corner nearest the postoffice in the Village of Liver-and-Onions.

Any Ice Today came along and said, "It looks like it used to be an 18 carat gold accordion with rich pawnshop diamonds in it; it looks like it used to be a grand accordion once and not so grand now."

"Oh, yes, oh, yes, it was gold all over on the outside," said the Potato Face Blind Man, "and

41

there was a diamond rabbit next to the handles on each side, two diamond rabbits."

"How do you mean diamond rabbits?" Any Ice Today asked.

"Ears, legs, head, feet, ribs, tail, all fixed out in diamonds to make a nice rabbit with his diamond chin on his diamond toenails. When I play good pieces so people cry hearing my accordion music, then I put my fingers over and feel of the rabbit's diamond chin on his diamond toenails, 'Attaboy, li'l bunny, attaboy, li'l bunny.'"

"Yes I hear you talking but it is like dream talking. I wonder why your accordion looks like somebody stole it and took it to a pawnshop and took it out and somebody stole it again and took it to a pawnshop and took it out and somebody stole it again. And they kept on stealing it and taking it out of the pawnshop and stealing it again till the gold wore off so it looks like a used-to-be-yesterday."

"Oh, yes, o-h, y-e-s, you are right. It is not

42

like the accordion it used to be. It knows more knowledge than it used to know just the same as this Potato Face Blind Man knows more knowledge than he used to know."

"Tell me about it," said Any Ice Today.

"It is simple. If a blind man plays an accordion on the street to make people cry it makes them sad and when they are sad the gold goes away off the accordion. And if a blind man goes to sleep because his music is full of sleepy songs like the long wind in a sleepy valley, then while the blind man is sleeping the diamonds in the diamond rabbit all go away. I play a sleepy song and go to sleep and I wake up and the diamond ear of the diamond rabbit is gone. I play another sleepy song and go to sleep and wake up and the diamond tail of the diamond rabbit is gone. After a while all the diamond rabbits are gone, even the diamond chin sitting on the diamond toenails of the rabbits next to the handles of the accordion, even those are gone."

43

"Is there anything I can do?" asked Any Ice Today.

"I do it myself," said the Potato Face Blind Man. "If I am too sorry I just play the sleepy song of the long wind going up the sleepy valleys. And that carries me away where I have time and money to dream about the new wonderful accordions and postoffices where everybody that gets a letter and everybody that don't get a letter stops and remembers the Potato Face Blind Man."

How the Potato Face Blind Man Enjoyed Himself on a Fine Spring Morning

On a Friday morning when the flummywisters were yodeling yisters high in the elm trees, the Potato Face Blind Man came down to his work sitting at the corner nearest the postoffice in the Village of Liver-and-Onions and playing his gold-that-used-to-be accordion for the pleasure of the ears of the people going into the postoffice to see if they got any letters for themselves or their families.

"It is a good day, a lucky day," said the Potato Face Blind Man, "because for a beginning I have heard high in the elm trees the flummywisters yodeling their yisters in the long branches of the lingering leaves. So—so— I am going to listen to myself playing on my accordion the same yisters, the same yodels, drawing them like long glad breathings out of my glad accordion, long breathings of the branches of the lingering leaves."

And he sat down in his chair. On the sleeve of his coat he tied a sign, "I Am Blind *Too*." On the top button of his coat he hung a little thimble. On the bottom button of his coat he hung a tin copper cup. On the middle button he hung a wooden mug. By the side of him on the left side on the sidewalk he put a galvanized iron washtub, and on the right side an aluminum dishpan.

"It is a good day, a lucky day, and I am sure many people will stop and remember the Potato Face Blind Man," he sang to himself like a little song as he began running his fingers up and down the keys of the accordion like the

46

"I am sure many people will stop and remember the
Potato Face Blind Man"

yisters of the lingering leaves in the elm trees.

Then came Pick Ups. Always it happened Pick Ups asked questions and wished to know. And so this is how the questions and answers ran when the Potato Face filled the ears of Pick Ups with explanations.

"What is the piece you are playing on the keys of your accordion so fast sometimes, so slow sometimes, so sad some of the moments, so glad some of the moments?"

"It is the song the mama flummywisters sing when they button loose the winter underwear of the baby flummywisters and sing:

"Fly, you little flummies,
Sing, you little wisters."

"And why do you have a little thimble on the top button of your coat?"

"That is for the dimes to be put in. Some people see it and say, 'Oh, I must put in a whole thimbleful of dimes.' "

"And the tin copper cup?"

49

"That is for the base ball players to stand off ten feet and throw in nickels and pennies. The one who throws the most into the cup will be the most lucky."

"And the wooden mug?"

"There is a hole in the bottom of it. The hole is as big as the bottom. The nickel goes in and comes out again. It is for the very poor people who wish to give me a nickel and yet get the nickel back."

"The aluminum dishpan and the galvanized iron washtub—what are they doing by the side of you on both sides on the sidewalk?"

"Sometime maybe it will happen everybody who goes into the postoffice and comes out will stop and pour out all their money, because they might get afraid their money is no good any more. If such a happening ever happens then it will be nice for the people to have some place to pour their money. Such is the explanation why you see the aluminum dishpan and galvanized iron tub."

"Explain your sign—why is it, 'I Am Blind *Too.*' "

"Oh, I am sorry to explain to you, Pick Ups, why this is so which. Some of the people who pass by here going into the postoffice and coming out, they have eyes—but they see nothing with their eyes. They look where they are going and they get where they wish to get, but they forget why they came and they do not know how to come away. They are my blind brothers. It is for them I have the sign that reads, 'I Am Blind *Too.*' "

"I have my ears full of explanations and I thank you," said Pick Ups.

"Good-by," said the Potato Face Blind Man as he began drawing long breathings like lingering leaves out of the accordion—along with the song the mama flummywisters sing when they button loose the winter underwear of the baby flummywisters.

Poker Face the Baboon and Hot Dog the Tiger

When the moon has a green rim with red meat inside and black seeds on the red meat, then in the Rootabaga Country they call it a Watermelon Moon and look for anything to happen.

It was a night when a Watermelon Moon was shining. Lizzie Lazarus came to the upstairs room of the Potato Face Blind Man. Poker Face the Baboon and Hot Dog the Tiger were with her. She was leading them with a pink string.

"You see they are wearing pajamas," she said. "They sleep with you to-night and to-morrow they go to work with you like mascots."

"How like mascots?" asked the Potato Face Blind Man.

"They are luck bringers. They keep your good luck if it is good. They change your bad luck if it is bad."

"I hear you and my ears get your explanations."

So the next morning when the Potato Face Blind Man sat down to play his accordion on the corner nearest the postoffice in the Village of Liver-and-Onions, next to him on the right hand side sitting on the sidewalk was Poker Face the Baboon and on the left hand side sitting next to him was Hot Dog the Tiger.

They looked like dummies—they were so quiet. They looked as if they were made of wood and paper and then painted. In the eyes of Poker Face was something faraway.

54

In the eyes of Hot Dog was something hungry. Whitson Whimble, the patent clothes wringer manufacturer, came by in his big limousine automobile car without horses to pull it. He was sitting back on the leather upholstered seat cushions.

"Stop here," he commanded the chauffeur driving the car.

Then Whitson Whimble sat looking. First he looked into the eyes of Poker Face the Baboon and saw something faraway. Then he looked into the eyes of Hot Dog the Tiger and saw something hungry. Then he read the sign painted by the Potato Face Blind Man saying, "You look at 'em and see 'em; I look at 'em and I don't. You watch what their eyes say; I can only feel their hair." Then Whitson Whimble commanded the chauffeur driving the car, "Go on."

Fifteen minutes later a man in overalls came down Main Street with a wheelbarrow. He stopped in front of the Potato Face Blind Man,

Poker Face the Baboon, and Hot Dog the Tiger.

"Where is the aluminum dishpan?" he asked.

"On my left side on the sidewalk," answered the Potato Face Blind Man.

"Where is the galvanized iron washtub?"

"On my right side on the sidewalk."

Then the man in overalls took a shovel and began shoveling silver dollars out of the wheelbarrow into the aluminum dishpan and the galvanized iron washtub. He shoveled out of the wheelbarrow till the dishpan was full, till the washtub was full. Then he put the shovel into the wheelbarrow and went up Main Street.

Six o'clock that night Pick Ups came along. The Potato Face Blind Man said to him, "I have to carry home a heavy load of money tonight, an aluminum dishpan full of silver dollars and a galvanized iron washtub full of silver dollars. So I ask you, will you take care of Poker Face the Baboon and Hot Dog the Tiger?"

"Yes," said Pick Ups, "I will." And he did. He tied a pink string to their legs and took them home and put them in the woodshed.

Poker Face the Baboon went to sleep on the soft coal at the north end of the woodshed and when he was asleep his face had something faraway in it and he was so quiet he looked like a dummy with brown hair of the jungle painted on his black skin and a black nose painted on his brown face. Hot Dog the Tiger went to sleep on the hard coal at the south end of the woodshed and when he was asleep his eyelashes had something hungry in them and he looked like a painted dummy with black stripes painted over his yellow belly and a black spot painted away at the end of his long yellow tail.

In the morning the woodshed was empty. Pick Ups told the Potato Face Blind Man, "They left a note in their own handwriting on perfumed pink paper. It said, *'Mascots never stay long.'*"

And that is why for many years the Potato

57

Face Blind Man had silver dollars to spend—
and that is why many people in the Rootabaga
Country keep their eyes open for a Watermelon
Moon in the sky with a green rim and red meat
inside and black seeds making spots on the red
meat.

The Toboggan-to-the-Moon Dream of the Potato Face Blind Man

One morning in October the Potato Face Blind Man sat on the corner nearest the postoffice.

Any Ice Today came along and said, "This is the sad time of the year."

"Sad?" asked the Potato Face Blind Man, changing his accordion from his right knee to his left knee, and singing softly to the tune he was fumbling on the accordion keys, "Be Happy in the Morning When the Birds Bring the Beans."

"Yes," said Any Ice Today, "is it not sad

every year when the leaves change from green to yellow, when the leaves dry on the branches and fall into the air, and the wind blows them and they make a song saying, 'Hush baby, hush baby,' and the wind fills the sky with them and they are like a sky full of birds who forget they know any songs."

"It is sad and not sad," was the blind man's word.

"Listen," said the Potato Face. "For me this is the time of the year when the dream of the white moon toboggan comes back. Five weeks before the first snow flurry this dream always comes back to me. It says, 'The black leaves are falling now and they fill the sky but five weeks go by and then for every black leaf there will be a thousand snow crystals shining white.'"

"What was your dream of the white moon toboggan?" asked Any Ice Today.

"It came to me first when I was a boy, when I had my eyes, before my luck changed. I saw

60

the big white spiders of the moon working, rushing around climbing up, climbing down, snizzling and sniffering. I looked a long while before I saw what the big white spiders on the moon were doing. I saw after a while they were weaving a long toboggan, a white toboggan, white and soft as snow. And after a long while of snizzling and sniffering, climbing up and climbing down, at last the toboggan was done, a snow white toboggan running from the moon down to the Rootabaga Country.

"And sliding, sliding down from the moon on this toboggan were the White Gold Boys and the Blue Silver Girls. They tumbled down at my feet because, you see, the toboggan ended right at my feet. I could lean over and pick up the White Gold Boys and the Blue Silver Girls as they slid out of the toboggan at my feet. I could pick up a whole handful of them and hold them in my hand and talk with them. Yet, you understand, whenever I tried to shut my hand and keep any of them they would snizzle and sniffer and jump out of the cracks between my fingers. Once there was a little gold and silver dust on my left hand thumb, dust they snizzled out while slipping away from me.

"Once I heard a White Gold Boy and a Blue Silver Girl whispering. They were standing on the tip of my right hand little finger, whispering. One said, 'I got pumpkins—what did you get?' The other said, 'I got hazel nuts.' I listened more and I found out there are millions of pumpkins and millions of hazel nuts so small you and I can not see them. These children from the moon, however, they can see them and whenever they slide down on the moon toboggan they take back their pockets full of things so little we have never seen them."

"They are wonderful children," said Any Ice Today. "And will you tell me how they get back to the moon after they slide down the toboggan?"

"Oh, that is easy," said Potato Face. "It is just as easy for them to slide *up* to the moon as to slide down. Sliding up and sliding down is the same for them. The big white spiders fixed it that way when they snizzled and sniffered and made the toboggan."

How Gimme the Ax Found Out About the Zigzag Railroad and Who Made It Zigzag

One day Gimme the Ax said to himself, "To-day I go to the postoffice and around, looking around. Maybe I will hear about something happening last night when I was sleeping. Maybe a policeman began laughing and fell in a cistern and came out with a wheelbarrow full of goldfish wearing new jewelry. How do I know? Maybe the man in the moon going down a cellar stairs to get a pitcher of butter-milk for the woman in the moon to drink and stop crying, maybe he fell down the stairs and broke the pitcher and laughed and picked up the broken pieces and said to himself, 'One, two, three, four, accidents happen in the best regulated families.' How do I know?"

So with his mind full of simple and refreshing thoughts, Gimme the Ax went out into the backyard garden and looked at the different necktie poppies growing early in the summer. Then he picked one of the necktie poppies to wear for a necktie scarf going downtown to the postoffice and around looking around.

"It is a good speculation to look nice around looking around in a necktie scarf," said Gimme the Ax. "It is a necktie with a picture like whiteface pony spots on a green frog swimming in the moonshine."

So he went downtown. For the first time he saw the Potato Face Blind Man playing an accordion on the corner next nearest the postoffice. He asked the Potato Face to tell him why the railroad tracks run zigzag in the Rootabaga Country.

Found Out About the Zigzag Railroad

"Long ago," said the Potato Face Blind Man, "long before the necktie poppies began growing in the backyard, long before there was a necktie scarf like yours with whiteface pony spots on a green frog swimming in the moonshine, back in the old days when they laid the rails for the railroad they laid the rails straight."

"Then the zizzies came. The zizzy is a bug. He runs zigzag on zigzag legs, eats zigzag with zigzag teeth, and spits zigzag with a zigzag tongue.

"Millions of zizzies came hizzing with little hizzers on their heads and under their legs. They jumped on the rails with their zigzag legs, and spit and twisted with their zigzag teeth and tongues till they twisted the whole railroad and all the rails and tracks into a zigzag railroad with zigzag rails for the trains, the passenger trains and the freight trains, all to run zigzag on.

"Then the zizzies crept away into the fields

67

where they sleep and cover themselves with zigzag blankets on special zigzag beds.

"Next day came shovelmen with their shovels, smooth engineers with smooth blue prints, and water boys with water pails and water dippers for the shovelmen to drink after shoveling the railroad straight. And I nearly forgot to say the steam and hoist operating engineers came and began their steam hoist and operating to make the railroad straight.

"They worked hard. They made the railroad straight again. They looked at the job and said to themselves and to each other, 'This is it—we done it.'

"Next morning the zizzies opened their zigzag eyes and looked over to the railroad and the rails. When they saw the railroad all straight again, and the rails and the ties and the spikes all straight again, the zizzies didn't even eat breakfast that morning.

"They jumped out of their zigzag beds,

jumped onto the rails with their zigzag legs and spit and twisted till they spit and twisted all the rails and the ties and the spikes back into a zigzag like the letter Z and the letter Z at the end of the alphabet.

"After that the zizzies went to breakfast. And they said to themselves and to each other, the same as the shovelmen, the smooth engineers and the steam hoist and operating engineers, 'This is it—we done it.'"

"So that is the how of the which—it was the zizzies," said Gimme the Ax.

"Yes, it was the zizzies," said the Potato Face Blind Man. "That is the story told to me."

"Who told it to you?"

"*Two little zizzies.* They came to me one cold winter night and slept in my accordion where the music keeps it warm in winter. In the morning I said, 'Good morning, zizzies, did you have a good sleep last night and pleasant dreams?' And after they had breakfast they told me the story. Both told it zigzag but it was the same kind of zigzag each had together."

3. Three Stories About the Gold Buckskin Whincher

People: Blixie Bimber
Peter Potato Blossom Wishes
Jimmie the Flea
Silas Baxby
Fritz Axenbax
James Sixbixdix
Jason Squiff, the Cistern Cleaner
Rags Habakuk, the Rag Man
Two Daughters of the Rag Man
Two Blue Rats
A Circus Man With Spot Cash
A Moving Picture Actor
A Taxicab Driver

The Story of Blixie Bimber and the Power of the Gold Buckskin Whincher

Blixie Bimber grew up looking for luck. If she found a horseshoe she took it home and put it on the wall of her room with a ribbon tied to it. She would look at the moon through her fingers, under her arms, over her right shoulder but never—never over her *left* shoulder. She listened and picked up everything anybody said about the ground hog and whether the ground hog saw his shadow when he came out the second of February.

If she dreamed of onions she knew the next day she would find a silver spoon. If she dreamed of fishes she knew the next day she would meet a strange man who would call her by her first name. She grew up looking for luck.

She was sixteen years old and quite a girl, with her skirts down to her shoe tops, when something happened. She was going to the postoffice to see if there was a letter for her from Peter Potato Blossom Wishes, her best chum, or a letter from Jimmy the Flea, her best friend she kept steady company with.

Jimmy the Flea was a climber. He climbed skyscrapers and flagpoles and smokestacks and was a famous steeplejack. Blixie Bimber liked him because he was a steeplejack, a little, but more because he was a whistler.

Every time Blixie said to Jimmy, "I got the blues—whistle the blues out of me," Jimmy would just naturally whistle till the blues just naturally went away from Blixie.

On the way to the postoffice, Blixie found a gold buckskin *whincher*. There it lay in the middle of the sidewalk. How and why it came to be there she never knew and nobody ever told her. "It's luck," she said to herself as she picked it up quick.

And so—she took it home and fixed it on a little chain and wore it around her neck.

She did not know and nobody ever told her a gold buckskin whincher is different from just a plain common whincher. It has a *power*. And if a thing has a power over you then you just naturally can't help yourself.

So—around her neck fixed on a little chain Blixie Bimber wore the gold buckskin whincher and never knew it had a power and all the time the power was working.

"The first man you meet with an X in his name you must fall head over heels in love with him," said the silent power in the gold buckskin whincher.

And that was why Blixie Bimber stopped at the postoffice and went back again asking the clerk at the postoffice window if he was sure there wasn't a letter for her. The name of the clerk was Silas Baxby. For six weeks he kept steady company with Blixie Bimber. They went to dances, hayrack rides, picnics and high jinks together.

All the time the power in the gold buckskin whincher was working. It was hanging by a little chain around her neck and always working. It was saying, "The next man you meet with two X's in his name you must leave all and fall head over heels in love with him."

She met the high school principal. His name was Fritz Axenbax. Blixie dropped her eyes before him and threw smiles at him. And for six weeks he kept steady company with Blixie Bimber. They went to dances, hayrack rides, picnics and high jinks together.

"Why do you go with him for steady company?" her relatives asked.

"It's a power he's got," Blixie answered, "I just can't help it—it's a power."

"One of his feet is bigger than the other—

how can you keep steady company with him?" they asked again.

All she would answer was, "It's a power."

All the time, of course, the gold buckskin whincher on the little chain around her neck was working. It was saying, "If she meets a man with three X's in his name she must fall head over heels in love with him."

At a band concert in the public square one night she met James Sixbixdix. There was no helping it. She dropped her eyes and threw her smiles at him. And for six weeks they kept steady company going to band concerts, dances, hayrack rides, picnics and high jinks together.

"Why do you keep steady company with him? He's a musical soup eater," her relatives said to her. And she answered, "It's a power—I can't help myself."

Leaning down with her head in a rain water cistern one day, listening to the echoes against

77

the strange wooden walls of the cistern, the gold buckskin whincher on the little chain around her neck slipped off and fell down into the rain water.

"My luck is gone," said Blixie. Then she went into the house and made two telephone calls. One was to James Sixbixdix telling him she couldn't keep the date with him that night. The other was to Jimmy the Flea, the climber, the steeplejack.

"Come on over—I got the blues and I want you to whistle 'em away," was what she telephoned Jimmy the Flea.

And so—if you ever come across a gold buckskin whincher, be careful. It's got a power. It'll make you fall head over heels in love with the next man you meet with an X in his name. Or it will do other strange things because different whinchers have different powers.

The Story of Jason Squiff and Why He Had a Popcorn Hat, Popcorn Mittens and Popcorn Shoes

Jason Squiff was a cistern cleaner. He had greenish yellowish hair. If you looked down into a cistern when he was lifting buckets of slush and mud you could tell where he was, you could pick him out down in the dark cistern, by the lights of his greenish yellowish hair.

Sometimes the buckets of slush and mud tipped over and ran down on the top of his head. This covered his greenish yellowish hair. And then it was hard to tell where he was and it was

79

not easy to pick him out down in the dark where he was cleaning the cistern.

One day Jason Squiff came to the Bimber house and knocked on the door.

"Did I understand," he said, speaking to Mrs. Bimber, Blixie Bimber's mother, "do I understand you sent for me to clean the cistern in your back yard?"

"You understand exactly such," said Mrs. Bimber, "and you are welcome as the flowers that bloom in the spring, tra-la-la."

"Then I will go to work and clean the cistern, tra-la-la," he answered, speaking to Mrs. Bimber. "I'm the guy, tra-la-la," he said further, running his excellent fingers through his greenish yellowish hair which was shining brightly.

He began cleaning the cistern. Blixie Bimber came out in the back yard. She looked down in the cistern. It was all dark. It looked like nothing but all dark down there. By and by she saw something greenish yellowish. She

80

watched it. Soon she saw it was Jason Squiff's head and hair. And then she knew the cistern was being cleaned and Jason Squiff was on the job. So she sang tra-la-la and went back into the house and told her mother Jason Squiff was on the job.

The last bucketful of slush and mud came at last for Jason Squiff. He squinted at the bottom. Something was shining. He reached his fingers down through the slush and mud and took out what was shining.

It was the gold buckskin whincher Blixie Bimber lost from the gold chain around her neck the week before when she was looking down into the cistern to see what she could see. It was exactly the same gold buckskin whincher shining and glittering like a sign of happiness.

"It's luck," said Jason Squiff, wiping his fingers on his greenish yellowish hair. Then he put the gold buckskin whincher in his vest pocket and spoke to himself again, "It's luck."

A little after six o'clock that night Jason

Squiff stepped into his house and home and said hello to his wife and daughters. They all began to laugh. Their laughter was a ticklish laughter.

"Something funny is happening," he said.

"And you are it," they all laughed at him again with ticklish laughter.

Then they showed him. His hat was popcorn, his mittens popcorn and his shoes popcorn. He didn't know the gold buckskin whincher had a power and was working all the time. He didn't know the whincher in his vest pocket was saying, "You have a letter Q in your name and because you have the pleasure and happiness of having a Q in your name you must have a popcorn hat, popcorn mittens and popcorn shoes."

The next morning he put on another hat, another pair of mittens and another pair of shoes. And the minute he put them on they changed to popcorn.

So he tried on all his hats, mittens and shoes.

His hat was popcorn, his mittens popcorn and his
shoes popcorn

Always they changed to popcorn the minute he had them on.

He went downtown to the stores. He bought a new hat, mittens and shoes. And the minute he had them on they changed to popcorn.

So he decided he would go to work and clean cisterns with his popcorn hat, popcorn mittens and popcorn shoes on.

The people of the Village of Cream Puffs enjoyed watching him walk up the street, going to clean cisterns. People five and six blocks away could see him coming and going with his popcorn hat, popcorn mittens and popcorn shoes.

When he was down in a cistern the children enjoyed looking down into the cistern to see him work. When none of the slush and mud fell on his hat and mittens he was easy to find. The light of the shining popcorn lit up the whole inside of the cistern.

Sometimes, of course, the white popcorn got

full of black slush and black mud. And then when Jason Squiff came up and walked home he was not quite so dazzling to look at.

It was a funny winter for Jason Squiff.

"It's a crime, a dirty crime," he said to himself. "Now I can never be alone with my thoughts. Everybody looks at me when I go up the street."

"If I meet a funeral even the pall bearers begin to laugh at my popcorn hat. If I meet people going to a wedding they throw all the rice at me as if I am a bride and a groom all together.

"The horses try to eat my hat wherever I go. Three hats I have fed to horses this winter.

"And if I accidentally drop one of my mittens the chickens eat it."

Then Jason Squiff began to change. He became proud.

"I always wanted a white beautiful hat like this white popcorn hat," he said to himself.

86

"And I always wanted white beautiful mittens and white beautiful shoes like these white popcorn mittens and shoes."

When the boys yelled, "Snow man! yah-de-dah-de-dah, Snow man!" he just waved his hand to them with an upward gesture of his arm to show he was proud of how he looked.

"They all watch for me," he said to himself, "I am distinquished—am I not?" he asked himself.

And he put his right hand into his left hand and shook hands with himself and said, "You certainly look fixed up."

One day he decided to throw away his vest. In the vest pocket was the gold buckskin whincher, with the power working, the power saying, "You have a letter Q in your name and because you have the pleasure and happiness of having a Q in your name you must have a popcorn hat, popcorn mittens and popcorn shoes."

Yes, he threw away the vest. He forgot all about the gold buckskin whincher being in the vest.

He just handed the vest to a rag man. And the rag man put the vest with the gold buckskin whincher in a bag on his back and walked away.

After that Jason Squiff was like other people. His hats would never change to popcorn nor his mittens to popcorn nor his shoes to popcorn.

And when anybody looked at him down in a cistern cleaning the cistern or when anybody saw him walking along the street they knew him by his greenish yellowish hair which was always full of bright lights.

And so—if you have a Q in your name, be careful if you ever come across a gold buckskin whincher. Remember different whinchers have different powers.

The Story of Rags Habakuk, the Two Blue Rats, and the Circus Man Who Came with Spot Cash Money

Rags Habakuk was going home. His day's work was done. The sun was down. Street lamps began shining. Burglars were starting on their night's work. It was no time for an honest ragman to be knocking on people's back doors, saying, "Any rags?" or else saying, "Any rags? any bottles? any bones?" or else saying "Any rags? any bottles? any bones? any old iron? any copper, brass, old shoes all run down and no good to anybody to-day? any old clothes, old coats, pants, vests? I take any old clothes you got."

Yes, Rags Habakuk was going home. In the gunnysack bag on his back, humped up on top of the rag humps in the bag, was an old vest. It was the same old vest Jason Squiff threw out of a door at Rags Habakuk. In the pocket of the vest was the gold buckskin whincher with a power in it.

Well, Rags Habakuk got home just like always, sat down to supper and smacked his mouth and had a big supper of fish, just like always. Then he went out to a shanty in the back yard and opened up the gunnysack rag bag and fixed things out classified just like every day when he came home he opened the gunnysack bag and fixed things out classified.

The last thing of all he fixed out classified was the vest with the gold buckskin whincher in the pocket. "Put it on—it's a glad rag," he said, looking at the vest. "It's a lucky vest." So he put his right arm in the right armhole and his left arm in the left armhole. And there he was with his arms in the armholes of the old vest all fixed out classified new.

Next morning Rags Habakuk kissed his wife g'by and his eighteen year old girl g'by and his nineteen year old girl g'by. He kissed them just like he always kissed them—in a hurry—and as he kissed each one he said, "I will be back soon if not sooner and when I come back I will return."

Yes, up the street went Rags Habakuk. And soon as he left home something happened. Standing on his right shoulder was a blue rat and standing on his left shoulder was a blue rat. The only way he knew they were there was by looking at them.

There they were, close to his ears. He could feel the far edge of their whiskers against his ears.

"This never happened to me before all the time I been picking rags," he said. "Two blue rats stand by my ears and never say anything even if they know I am listening to anything they tell me."

So Rags Habakuk walked on two blocks, three blocks, four blocks, squinting with his right eye slanting at the blue rat on his right shoulder and squinting with his left eye slanting at the blue rat on his left shoulder.

"If I stood on somebody's shoulder with my whiskers right up in somebody's ear I would say something for somebody to listen to," he muttered.

Of course, he did not understand it was the gold buckskin whincher and the power working. Down in the pocket of the vest he had on, the gold buckskin whincher power was saying, "Because you have two K's in your name you must have two blue rats on your shoulders, one blue rat for your right ear, one blue rat for your left ear."

It was good business. Never before did Rags Habakuk get so much old rags.

Blue Rats and the Circus Man

"Come again—you and your lucky blue rats," people said to him. They dug into their cellars and garrets and brought him bottles and bones and copper and brass and old shoes and old clothes, coats, pants, vests.

Every morning when he went up the street with the two blue rats on his shoulders, blinking their eyes straight ahead and chewing their whiskers so they sometimes tickled the ears of old Rags Habakuk, sometimes women came running out on the front porch to look at him and say, "Well, if he isn't a queer old mysterious ragman and if those ain't queer old mysterious blue rats!"

All the time the gold buckskin whincher and the power was working. It was saying, "So long as old Rags Habakuk keeps the two blue rats he shall have good luck—but if he ever sells one of the blue rats then one of his daughters shall marry a taxicab driver—and if he ever sells the other blue rat then his other daughter shall marry a moving-picture hero actor."

Then terrible things happened. A circus man came. "I give you one thousand dollars spot cash money for one of the blue rats," he expostulated with his mouth. "And I give you two thousand dollars spot cash money for the two of the blue rats both of them together."

"Show me how much spot cash money two thousand dollars is all counted out in one pile for one man to carry away home in his gunny-sack rag bag," was the answer of Rags Habakuk.

The circus man went to the bank and came back with spot cash greenbacks money.

"This spot cash greenbacks money is made from the finest silk rags printed by the national government for the national republic to make business rich and prosperous," said the circus man, expostulating with his mouth.

"T-h-e f-i-n-e-s-t s-i-l-k r-a-g-s," he expostulated again holding two fingers under the nose of Rags Habakuk.

"I take it," said Rags Habakuk, "I take it. It is a whole gunnysack bag full of spot cash greenbacks money. I tell my wife it is printed by the national government for the national republic to make business rich and prosperous."

Then he kissed the blue rats, one on the right ear, the other on the left ear, and handed them over to the circus man.

And that was why the next month his eighteen year old daughter married a taxicab driver who was so polite all the time to his customers that he never had time to be polite to his wife.

And that was why his nineteen year old daughter married a moving-picture hero actor who worked so hard being nice and kind in the moving pictures that he never had enough left over for his wife when he got home after the day's work.

The Story of Rags Habakuk

And the lucky vest with the gold buckskin whincher was stolen from Rags Habakuk by the taxicab driver.

4. Four Stories About the Deep Doom of Dark Doorways

People: The Rag Doll
The Broom Handle
Spoon Lickers
Chocolate Chins
Dirty Bibs
Tin Pan Bangers
Clean Ears
Easy Ticklers
Musical Soup Eaters
Chubby Chubs
Sleepy Heads

Snoo Foo
Blink, Swink and Jink
Blunk, Swunk and Junk
Missus Sniggers

Eeta Peeca Pie
Meeny Miney
Miney Mo
A Potato Bug Millionaire

Bimbo the Snip
Bevo the Hike
A Ward Alderman
A Barn Boss
A Weather Man
A Traffic Policeman
A Monkey
A Widow Woman
An Umbrella Handle Maker

The Wedding Procession of the Rag Doll and the Broom Handle and Who Was in It

The Rag Doll had many friends. The Whisk Broom, the Furnace Shovel, the Coffee Pot, they all liked the Rag Doll very much.

But when the Rag Doll married, it was the Broom Handle she picked because the Broom Handle fixed her eyes.

A proud child, proud but careless, banged the head of the Rag Doll against a door one day and knocked off both the glass eyes sewed on

99

long ago. It was then the Broom Handle found two black California prunes, and fastened the two California prunes just where the eyes belonged. So then the Rag Doll had two fine black eyes brand new. She was even nicknamed Black Eyes by some people.

There was a wedding when the Rag Doll married the Broom Handle. It was a grand wedding with one of the grandest processions ever seen at a rag doll wedding. And we are sure no broom handle ever had a grander wedding procession when he got married.

Who marched in the procession? Well, first came the Spoon Lickers. Every one of them had a tea spoon, or a soup spoon, though most of them had a big table spoon. On the spoons, what did they have? Oh, some had butter scotch, some had gravy, some had marshmallow fudge. Every one had something slickery sweet or fat to eat on the spoon. And as they marched in the wedding procession of the Rag Doll and the Broom Handle, they licked their spoons and

100

looked around and licked their spoons again.

Next came the Tin Pan Bangers. Some had dishpans, some had frying pans, some had potato peeling pans. All the pans were tin with tight tin bottoms. And the Tin Pan Bangers banged with knives and forks and iron and wooden bangers on the bottoms of the tin pans. And as they marched in the wedding procession of the Rag Doll and the Broom Handle they banged their pans and looked around and banged again.

Then came the Chocolate Chins. They were all eating chocolates. And the chocolate was slippery and slickered all over their chins. Some of them spattered the ends of their noses with black chocolate. Some of them spread the brown chocolate nearly up to their ears. And then as they marched in the wedding procession of the Rag Doll and the Broom Handle they stuck their chins in the air and looked around and stuck their chins in the air again.

Then came the Dirty Bibs. They wore plain

white bibs, checker bibs, stripe bibs, blue bibs and bibs with butterflies. But all the bibs were dirty. The plain white bibs were dirty, the checker bibs were dirty, the stripe bibs, the blue bibs and the bibs with butterflies on them, they were all dirty. And so in the wedding procession of the Rag Doll and the Broom Handle, the Dirty Bibs marched with their dirty fingers on the bibs and they looked around and laughed and looked around and laughed again.

Next came the Clean Ears. They were proud. How they got into the procession nobody knows. Their ears were all clean. They were clean not only on the outside but they were clean on the inside. There was not a speck of dirt or dust or muss or mess on the inside nor the outside of their ears. And so in the wedding procession of the Rag Doll and the Broom Handle, they wiggled their ears and looked around and wiggled their ears again.

The Easy Ticklers were next in the procession. Their faces were shining. Their cheeks were like bars of new soap. Their ribs were strong and the meat and the fat was thick on their ribs. It was plain to see they were saying, "Don't tickle me because I tickle so easy." And as they marched in the wedding procession of the Rag Doll and the Broom Handle, they tickled themselves and laughed and looked around and tickled themselves again.

The music was furnished mostly by the Musical Soup Eaters. They marched with big bowls of soup in front of them and big spoons for eating the soup. They whistled and chuzzled and snozzled the soup and the noise they made could be heard far up at the head of the procession where the Spoon Lickers were marching. So they dipped their soup and looked around and dipped their soup again.

The Chubby Chubs were next. They were roly poly, round faced smackers and snoozers. They were not fat babies—oh no, oh no—not fat but just chubby and easy to squeeze. They marched on their chubby legs and chubby feet and chubbed their chubbs and looked around and chubbed their chubbs again.

The last of all in the wedding procession of the Rag Doll and the Broom Handle were the Sleepyheads. They were smiling and glad to be marching but their heads were slimpsing down and their smiles were half fading away and their eyes were half shut or a little more than half shut. They staggered just a little as though their feet were not sure where they were going. They were the Sleepyheads, the last of all, in the wedding procession of the Rag Doll and the Broom Handle and the Sleepyheads they never looked around at all.

It *was* a grand procession, don't you think so?

How the Hat Ashes Shovel Helped Snoo Foo

If you want to remember the names of all six of the Sniggers children, remember that the three biggest were named Blink, Swink and Jink but the three littlest ones were named Blunk, Swunk and Junk. One day last January the three biggest had a fuss with the three littlest. The fuss was about a new hat for Snoo Foo, the snow man, about what kind of a hat he should wear and how he should wear it. Blink, Swink and Jink said, "He wants a crooked hat put on straight." Blunk, Swunk and Junk said, "He wants a straight hat put on crooked." They fussed and fussed. Blink fussed with Blunk, Swink fussed with Swunk, and Jink fussed with Junk. The first ones to make up after the fuss were Jink and Junk. They decided the best way to settle the fuss. "Let's put a crooked hat on crooked," said Jink. "No, let's put a straight hat on straight," said Junk. Then they stood looking and looking into each other's shiny laughing eyes and then both of them exploded to each other at the same time, "Let's put on two hats, a crooked hat crooked and a straight hat straight."

Well, they looked around for hats. But there were not any hats anywhere, that is, no hats big enough for a snow man with a big head like Snoo Foo. So they went in the house and asked their mother for *the hat ashes shovel*. Of course, in most any other house, the mother would be all worried if six children came tramping and clomping in, banging the door and all six ejaculating to their mother at once, "Where is the hat ashes shovel?" But Missus Sniggers wasn't worried at all. She rubbed her chin with her finger and said softly, "Oh lah de dah, oh lah de dah, where is that hat ashes shovel, last week I had it when I was making a hat for Mister Sniggers; I remember I had that hat ashes shovel right up here over the clock, oh lah de dah, oh lah de dah. Go out and ring the front door bell," she said to Jink Sniggers. Jink ran away to the front door. And Missus Sniggers and the five children waited. Bling-bling the bell began ringing and—listen —the door of the clock opened and the hat ashes shovel fell out. "Oh lah de dah, get out of here in a hurry," said Missus Sniggers.

Well, the children ran out and dug a big pail of hat ashes with the hat ashes shovel. And they made two hats for Snoo Foo. One was a crooked hat. The other was a straight hat. And they put the crooked hat on crooked and the straight hat on straight. And there stood

How Snoo Foo Was Helped

Snoo Foo in the front yard and everybody who came by on the street, he would take off his hat to them, the crooked hat with his arm crooked and the straight hat with his arm straight. That was the end of the fuss between the Sniggers children and it was Jink, the littlest one of the biggest, and Junk, the littlest one of the littlest, who settled the fuss by looking clean into each other's eyes and laughing. If you ever get into a fuss try this way of settling it.

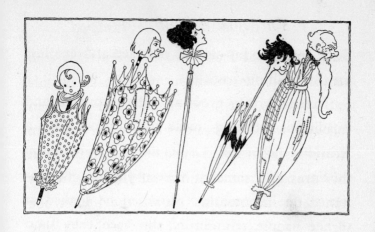

Three Boys With Jugs of Molasses and Secret Ambitions

In the Village of Liver-and-Onions, if *one* boy goes to the grocery for a jug of molasses it is just like always. And if *two* boys go to the grocery for a jug of molasses together it is just like always. But if *three* boys go to the grocery for a jug of molasses each and all together then it is not like always at all, at all.

Eeta Peeca Pie grew up with wishes and wishes working inside him. And for every wish inside him he had a freckle outside on his face. Whenever he smiled the smile ran way back into the far side of his face and got lost in the wishing freckles.

Meeny Miney grew up with suspicions and suspicions working inside him. And after a while some of the suspicions got fastened on his eyes and some of the suspicions got fastened on his mouth. So when he looked at other people straight in the face they used to say, "Meeny Miney looks so sad-like I wonder if he'll get by."

Miney Mo was different. He wasn't sad-like and suspicious like Meeny Miney. Nor was he full of wishes inside and freckles outside like Eeta Peeca Pie. He was all mixed up inside with wishes and suspicions. So he had a few freckles and a few suspicions on his face. When he looked other people straight in the face they used to say, "I don't know whether to laugh or cry."

So here we have 'em, three boys growing up with wishes, suspicions and mixed-up wishes and suspicions. They all looked different from each other. Each one, however, had a secret ambition. And all three had the same secret ambition.

An ambition is a little creeper that creeps and creeps in your heart night and day, singing a little song, "Come and find me, come and find me."

The secret ambition in the heart of Eeta Peeca Pie, Meeney Miney, and Miney Mo was an ambition to go railroading, to ride on railroad cars night and day, year after year. The whistles and the wheels of railroad trains were music to them.

Whenever the secret ambition crept in their hearts and made them too sad, so sad it was hard to live and stand for it, they would all three put their hands on each other's shoulder and sing the song of Joe. The chorus was like this:

> Joe, Joe, broke his toe,
> On the way to Mexico.
> Came back, broke his back,
> Sliding on the railroad track.

One fine summer morning all three mothers of all three boys gave each one a jug and said, "Go to the grocery and get a jug of molasses." All three got to the grocery at the same time. And all three went out of the door of the grocery together, each with a jug of molasses together and each with his secret ambition creeping around in his heart, all three together.

Two blocks from the grocery they stopped under a slippery elm tree. Eeta Peeca Pie was stretching his neck looking straight up into the slippery elm tree. He said it was always good for his freckles and it helped his wishes to stand under a slippery elm and look up.

While he was looking up his left hand let go the jug handle of the jug of molasses. And the jug went ka-flump, ka-flumpety-flump down on the stone sidewalk, cracked to pieces and let the molasses go running out over the sidewalk.

If you have never seen it, let me tell you molasses running out of a broken jug, over a stone

They stepped into the molasses with their bare feet

sidewalk under a slippery elm tree, looks peculiar and mysterious.

Eeta Peeca Pie stepped into the molasses with his bare feet. "It's a lotta fun," he said. "It tickles all over." So Meeney Miney and Miney Mo both stepped into the molasses with their bare feet.

Then what happened just happened. One got littler. Another got littler. All three got littler.

"You look to me only big as a potato bug," said Eeta Peeca Pie to Meeney Miney and Miney Mo. "It's the same like you look to us," said Meeney Miney and Miney Mo to Eeta Peeca Pie. And then because their secret ambition began to hurt them they all stood with hands on each other's shoulders and sang the Mexico Joe song.

Off the sidewalk they strolled, across a field of grass. They passed many houses of spiders and ants. In front of one house they saw Mrs.

Spider over a tub washing clothes for Mr. Spider.

"Why do you wear that frying pan on your head?" they asked her.

"In this country all ladies wear the frying pan on their head when they want a hat."

"But what if you want a hat when you are frying with the frying pan?" asked Eeta Peeca Pie.

"That never happens to any respectable lady in this country."

"Don't you never have no new style hats?" asked Meeney Miney.

"No, but we always have new style frying pans every spring and fall."

Hidden in the roots of a pink grass clump, they came to a city of twisted-nose spiders. On the main street was a store with a show window full of pink parasols. They walked in and said to the clerk, "We want to buy parasols."

"We don't sell parasols here," said the spider clerk.

"Well, lend us a parasol apiece," said all three.

"Gladly, most gladly," said the clerk.

"How do you do it?" asked Eeta.

"I don't have to," answered the spider clerk.

"How did it begin?"

"It never was otherwise."

"Don't you never get tired?"

"Every parasol is a joy."

"What do you do when the parasols are gone?"

"They always come back. These are the famous twisted-nose parasols made from the famous pink grass. You will lose them all, all three. Then they will all walk back to me here in this store on main street. I can not sell you something I know you will surely lose. Neither can I ask you to pay, for something you will forget, somewhere sometime, and when you forget it, it will walk back here to me again. Look—look!"

As he said "Look," the door opened and five

pink parasols came waltzing in and waltzed up into the show window.

"They always come back. Everybody forgets. Take your parasols and go. You will forget them and they will come back to me."

"He looks like he had wishes inside him," said Eeta Peeca Pie.

"He looks like he had suspicions," said Meeney Miney.

"He looks like he was all mixed up wishes and suspicions," said Miney Mo.

And once more because they all felt lonesome and their secret ambitions were creeping and eating, they put their hands on their shoulders and sang the Mexico Joe song.

Then came happiness. They entered the Potato Bug Country. And they had luck first of all the first hour they were in the Potato Bug Country. They met a Potato Bug millionaire.

"How are you a millionaire?" they asked him.

"Because I got a million," he answered.

"A million what?"

"A million *fleems*."

"Who wants fleems?"

"You want fleems if you're going to live here."

"Why so?"

"Because fleems is our money. In the Potato Bug Country, if you got no fleems you can't buy nothing nor anything. But if you got a million fleems you're a Potato Bug millionaire."

Then he surprised them.

"I like you because you got wishes and freckles," he said to Eeta Peeca Pie, filling the pockets of Eeta with fleems.

"And I like you because you got suspicions and you're sad-like," he said to Meeney Miney filling Meeney Miney's pockets full of fleems.

"And I like you because you got some wishes and some suspicions and you look mixed up," he said to Miney Mo, sticking handfuls and hand-fuls of fleems into the pockets of Miney Mo.

Wishes do come true. And suspicions do come true. Here they had been wishing all their lives, and had suspicions of what was going to happen, and now it all came true.

With their pockets filled with fleems they rode on all the railroad trains of the Potato Bug Country. They went to the railroad stations and bought tickets for the fast trains and the slow trains and even the trains that back up and run backward instead of where they start to go.

On the dining cars of the railroads of the Potato Bug Country they ate wonder ham from the famous Potato Bug Pigs, eggs from the Potato Bug Hens, et cetera.

It seemed to them they stayed a long while in the Potato Bug Country, years and years. Yes, the time came when all their fleems were gone. Then whenever they wanted a railroad ride or something to eat or a place to sleep, they put their hands on each other's shoulders and sang the Mexico Joe song. In the Potato Bug

Country they all said the Mexico Joe song was wonderful.

One morning while they were waiting to take an express train on the Early Ohio & Southwestern they sat near the roots of a big potato plant under the big green leaves. And far above them they saw a dim black cloud and they heard a shaking and a rustling and a spattering. They did not know it was a man of the Village of Liver-and-Onions. They did not know it was Mr. Sniggers putting paris green on the potato plants.

A big drop of paris green spattered down and fell onto the heads and shoulders of all three, Eeta Peeca Pie, Meeny Miney and Miney Mo.

Then what happened just happened. They got bigger and bigger—one, two, three. And when they jumped up and ran out of the potato rows, Mr. Sniggers thought they were boys playing tricks.

When they got home to their mothers and told all about the jug of molasses breaking on the stone sidewalk under the slippery elm tree, their mothers said it was careless. The boys said it was lucky because it helped them get their secret ambitions.

And a secret ambition is a little creeper that creeps and creeps in your heart night and day, singing a little song, "Come and find me, come and find me."

How Bimbo the Snip's Thumb Stuck to His Nose When the Wind Changed

Once there was a boy in the Village of Liver-and-Onions whose name was Bimbo the Snip. He forgot nearly everything his father and mother told him to do and told him not to do.

One day his father, Bevo the Hike, came home and found Bimbo the Snip sitting on the front steps with his thumb fastened to his nose and the fingers wiggling.

"I can't take my thumb away," said Bimbo the Snip, "because when I put my thumb to my nose and wiggled my fingers at the iceman the wind changed. And just like mother always said, if the wind changed the thumb would stay fastened to my nose and not come off."

Bevo the Hike took hold of the thumb and pulled. He tied a clothes line rope around it and pulled. He pushed with his foot and heel against it. And all the time the thumb stuck fast and the fingers wiggled from the end of the nose of Bimbo the Snip.

Bevo the Hike sent for the ward alderman. The ward alderman sent for the barn boss of the street cleaning department. The barn boss of the street cleaning department sent for the head vaccinator of the vaccination bureau of the health department. The head vaccinator of the vaccination bureau of the health department sent for the big main fixer of the weather bureau where they understand the tricks of the wind and the wind changing.

And the big main fixer of the weather bureau said, "If you hit the thumb six times with the end of a traffic policeman's club, the thumb will come loose."

So Bevo the Hike went to a traffic policeman standing on a street corner with a whistle telling the wagons and cars which way to go.

He told the traffic policeman, "The wind changed and Bimbo the Snip's thumb is fastened to his nose and will not come loose till it is hit six times with the end of a traffic policeman's club."

"I can't help you unless you find a monkey to take my place standing on the corner telling the wagons and cars which way to go," answered the traffic policeman.

So Bevo the Hike went to the zoo and said to a monkey, "The wind changed and Bimbo the Snip's thumb is fastened to his nose and will not come loose till it is hit with the end of a traffic policeman's club six times and the traffic policeman cannot leave his place on the street

125

corner telling the traffic which way to go unless a monkey comes and takes his place."

The monkey answered, "Get me a ladder with a whistle so I can climb up and whistle and tell the traffic which way to go."

So Bevo the Hike hunted and hunted over the city and looked and looked and asked and asked till his feet and his eyes and his head and his heart were tired from top to bottom.

Then he met an old widow woman whose husband had been killed in a sewer explosion when he was digging sewer ditches. And the old woman was carrying a bundle of picked-up kindling wood in a bag on her back because she did not have money enough to buy coal.

Bevo the Hike told her, "You have troubles. So have I. You are carrying a load on your back people can see. I am carrying a load and nobody sees it."

"Tell me your troubles," said the old widow woman. He told her. And she said, "In the next block is an old umbrella handle maker.

126

He has a ladder with a whistle. He climbs on the ladder when he makes long long umbrella handles. And he has the whistle on the ladder to be whistling."

Beyo the Hike went to the next block, found the house of the umbrella handle maker and said to him, "The wind changed and Bimbo the Snip's thumb is fastened to his nose and will not come loose till it is hit with the end of a traffic policeman's club six times and the traffic policeman cannot leave the corner where he is telling the traffic which way to go unless a monkey takes his place and the monkey cannot take his place unless he has a ladder with a whistle to stand on and whistle the wagons and cars which way to go."

Then the umbrella handle maker said, "To-night I have a special job because I must work on a long, long umbrella handle and I will need the ladder to climb up and the whistle to be whistling. But if you promise to have the ladder back by to-night you can take it."

127

Bimbo the Snip's Thumb

Bevo the Hike promised. Then he took the ladder with a whistle to the monkey, the monkey took the place of the traffic policeman while the traffic policeman went to the home of Bevo the Hike where Bimbo the Snip was sitting on the front steps with his thumb fastened to his nose wiggling his fingers at everybody passing by on the street.

The traffic policeman hit Bimbo the Snip's thumb five times with the club. And the thumb stuck fast. But the sixth time it was hit with the end of the traffic policeman's thumb club, it came loose.

Then Bevo thanked the policeman, thanked the monkey, and took the ladder with the whistle back to the umbrella handle maker's house and thanked him.

When Bevo the Hike got home that night Bimbo the Snip was in bed and all tickled. He said to his father, "I will be careful how I stick my thumb to my nose and wiggle my fingers the next time the wind changes."

The monkey took the place of the traffic policeman

5. Three Stories About Three Ways the Wind Went Winding

People: Two Skyscrapers
The Northwest Wind
The Golden Spike Limited Train
A Tin Brass Goat
A Tin Brass Goose
Newsies

Young Leather
Red Slippers
A Man to be Hanged
Five Jackrabbits

The Wooden Indian
The Shaghorn Buffalo
The Night Policeman

The Two Skyscrapers Who Decided to Have a Child

Two skyscrapers stood across the street from each other in the Village of Liver-and-Onions. In the daylight when the streets poured full of people buying and selling, these two skyscrapers talked with each other the same as mountains talk.

In the night time when all the people buying and selling were gone home and there were only policemen and taxicab drivers on the streets, in the night when a mist crept up the streets and threw a purple and gray wrapper over every-thing, in the night when the stars and the sky shook out sheets of purple and gray mist down over the town, then the two skyscrapers leaned toward each other and whispered.

Whether they whispered secrets to each other or whether they whispered simple things that you and I know and everybody knows, that is their secret. One thing is sure: they often were seen leaning toward each other and whispering in the night the same as mountains lean and whisper in the night.

High on the roof of one of the skyscrapers was a tin brass goat looking out across prairies, and silver blue lakes shining like blue porcelain breakfast plates, and out across silver snakes of winding rivers in the morning sun. And high on the roof of the other skyscraper was a tin brass goose looking out across prairies, and silver blue lakes shining like blue porcelain breakfast plates, and out across silver snakes of winding rivers in the morning sun.

Decided to Have a Child

Now the Northwest Wind was a friend of the two skyscrapers. Coming so far, coming five hundred miles in a few hours, coming so fast always while the skyscrapers were standing still, standing always on the same old street corners always, the Northwest Wind was a bringer of news.

"Well, I see the city is here yet," the Northwest Wind would whistle to the skyscrapers.

And they would answer, "Yes, and are the mountains standing yet way out yonder where you come from, Wind?"

"Yes, the mountains are there yonder, and farther yonder is the sea, and the railroads are still going, still running across the prairie to the mountains, to the sea," the Northwest Wind would answer.

And now there was a pledge made by the Northwest Wind to the two skyscrapers. Often the Northwest Wind shook the tin brass goat and shook the tin brass goose on top of the skyscrapers.

"Are you going to blow loose the tin brass goat on my roof?" one asked.

"Are you going to blow loose the tin brass goose on my roof?" the other asked.

"Oh, no," the Northwest Wind laughed, first to one and then to the other, "if I ever blow loose your tin brass goat and if I ever blow loose your tin brass goose, it will be when I am sorry for you because you are up against hard luck and there is somebody's funeral."

So time passed on and the two skyscrapers stood with their feet among the policemen and the taxicabs, the people buying and selling, —the customers with parcels, packages and bundles—while away high on their roofs stood the goat and the goose looking out on silver blue lakes like blue porcelain breakfast plates and silver snakes of rivers winding in the morning sun.

So time passed on and the Northwest Wind kept coming, telling the news and making promises.

Decided to Have a Child

So time passed on. And the two skyscrapers decided to have a child.

And they decided when their child came it should be a *free* child.

"It must be a free child," they said to each other. "It must not be a child standing still all its life on a street corner. Yes, if we have a child she must be free to run across the prairie, to the mountains, to the sea. Yes, it must be a free child."

So time passed on. Their child came. It was a railroad train, the Golden Spike Limited, the fastest long distance train in the Rootabaga Country. It ran across the prairie, to the mountains, to the sea.

They were glad, the two skyscrapers were, glad to have a free child running away from the big city, far away to the mountains, far away to the sea, running as far as the farthest mountains and sea coasts touched by the Northwest Wind.

They were glad their child was useful, the

two skyscrapers were, glad their child was carrying a thousand people a thousand miles a
day, so when people spoke of the Golden Spike
Limited, they spoke of it as a strong, lovely
child.

Then time passed on. There came a day
when the newsies yelled as though they were
crazy. "Yah yah, blah blah, yoh yoh," was
what it sounded like to the two skyscrapers who
never bothered much about what the newsies
were yelling.

"Yah yah, blah blah, yoh yoh," was the cry
of the newsies that came up again to the tops
of the skyscrapers.

At last the yelling of the newsies came so
strong the skyscrapers listened and heard the
newsies yammering, "All about the great train
wreck! All about the Golden Spike disaster!
Many lives lost! Many lives lost!"

And the Northwest Wind came howling a
slow sad song. And late that afternoon a crowd
of policemen, taxicab drivers, newsies and

customers with bundles, all stood around talking and wondering about two things next to each other on the street car track in the middle of the street. One was a tin brass goat. The other was a tin brass goose. And they lay next to each other.

The Dollar Watch and the Five Jack Rabbits

Long ago, long before the waylacks lost the wonderful stripes of oat straw gold and the spots of timothy hay green in their marvelous curving tail feathers, long before the doo-doo-jangers whistled among the honeysuckle blossoms and the bitter-basters cried their last and dying wrangling cries, long before the sad happenings that came later, it was then, some years earlier than the year Fifty Fifty, that Young Leather and Red Slippers crossed the Rootabaga Country.

To begin with, they were walking across the Rootabaga Country. And they were walking because it made their feet glad to feel the dirt of the earth under their shoes and they were close to the smells of the earth. They learned the ways of birds and bugs, why birds have wings, why bugs have legs, why the gladdy-whingers have spotted eggs in a basket nest in a booblow tree, and why the chizzywhizzies scrape off little fiddle songs all summer long while the summer nights last.

Early one morning they were walking across the corn belt of the Rootabaga Country singing, "Deep Down Among the Dagger Dancers." They had just had a breakfast of coffee and hot hankypank cakes covered with cow's butter. Young Leather said to Red Slippers, "What is the best secret we have come across this summer?"

"That is easy to answer," Red Slippers said with a long flish of her long black eyelashes. "The best secret we have come across is a rope of gold hanging from every star in the sky and when we want to go up we go up."

Walking on they came to a town where they met a man with a sorry face. "Why?" they asked him. And he answered, "My brother is in jail."

"What for?" they asked him again. And he answered again, "My brother put on a straw hat in the middle of the winter and went out on the streets laughing; my brother had his hair cut pompompadour and went out on the streets bareheaded in the summertime laughing; and these things were against the law. Worst of all he sneezed at the wrong time and he sneezed before the wrong persons; he sneezed when it was not wise to sneeze. So he will be hanged to-morrow morning. The gallows made of lumber and the rope made of hemp —they are waiting for him to-morrow morning. They will tie around his neck the hangman's necktie and hoist him high."

The man with a sorry face looked more sorry

143

than ever. It made Young Leather feel reck-less and it made Red Slippers feel reckless. They whispered to each other. Then Young Leather said, "Take this dollar watch. Give it to your brother. Tell him when they are leading him to the gallows he must take this dollar watch in his hand, wind it up and push on the stem winder. The rest will be easy."

So the next morning when they were leading the man to be hanged to the gallows made of lumber and the rope made of hemp, where they were going to hoist him high because he sneezed in the wrong place before the wrong people, he used his fingers winding up the watch and push-ing on the stem winder. There was a snapping and a slatching like a gas engine slipping into a big pair of dragon fly wings. The dollar watch changed into a dragon fly ship. The man who was going to be hanged jumped into the dragon fly ship and flew whonging away before anybody could stop him.

The Five Jack Rabbits

Young Leather and Red Slippers were walking out of the town laughing and singing again, "Deep Down Among the Dagger Dancers." The man with a sorry face, not so sorry now any more, came running after them. Behind the man and running after him were five long-legged spider jack-rabbits.

"These are for you," was his exclamation. And they all sat down on the stump of a boo-blow tree. He opened his sorry face and told the secrets of the five long-legged spider jack-rabbits to Young Leather and Red Slippers. They waved good-by and went on up the road leading the five new jack-rabbits.

In the next town they came to was a sky-scraper higher than all the other skyscrapers. A rich man dying wanted to be remembered and left in his last will and testament a command they should build a building so high it would scrape the thunder clouds and stand higher than all other skyscrapers with his name carved in stone letters on the top of it, and an electric sign at night with his name on it, and a clock on the tower with his name on it.

"I am hungry to be remembered and have my name spoken by many people after I am dead," the rich man told his friends. "I command you, therefore, to throw the building high in the air because the higher it goes the longer I will be remembered and the longer the years men will mention my name after I am dead."

So there it was. Young Leather and Red Slippers laughed when they first saw the skyscraper, when they were far off along a country road singing their old song, "Deep Down Among the Dagger Dancers."

"We got a show and we give a performance and we want the whole town to see it," was what Young Leather and Red Slippers said to the mayor of the town when they called on him at the city hall. "We want a license and a permit to give this free show in the public square."

"What do you do?" asked the mayor.

The Five Jack Rabbits

"We jump five jack-rabbits, five long-legged spider jack-rabbits over the highest skyscraper you got in your city," they answered him.

"If it's free and you don't sell anything nor take any money away from us while it is daylight and you are giving your performance, then here is your license permit," said the mayor speaking in the manner of a politician who has studied politics.

Thousands of people came to see the show on the public square. They wished to know how it would look to see five long-legged, spider jack-rabbits jump over the highest skyscraper in the city.

Four of the jack-rabbits had stripes. The fifth had stripes—and spots. Before they started the show Young Leather and Red Slippers held the jack-rabbits one by one in their arms and petted them, rubbed the feet and rubbed the long ears and ran their fingers along the long legs of the jumpers.

"Zingo," they yelled to the first jack-rabbit.

He got all ready. "And now zingo!" they yelled again. And the jack-rabbit took a run, lifted off his feet and went on and on and up and up till he went over the roof of the sky-scraper and then went down and down till he lit on his feet and came running on his long legs back to the public square where he started from, back where Young Leather and Red Slippers petted him and rubbed his long ears and said, "That's the boy."

Then three jack-rabbits made the jump over the skyscraper. "Zingo," they heard and got ready. "And now zingo," they heard and all three together in a row, their long ears touching each other, they lifted off their feet and went on and on and up and up till they cleared the roof of the skyscraper. Then they came down and down till they lit on their feet and came running to the hands of Young Leather and Red Slippers to have their long legs and their long ears rubbed and petted.

Then came the turn of the fifth jack-rabbit,

148

the beautiful one with stripes and spots. "Ah, we're sorry to see you go, Ah-h, we're sorry," they said, rubbing his long ears and feeling of his long legs.

Then Young Leather and Red Slippers kissed him on the nose, kissed the last and fifth of the five long-legged spider jack-rabbits.

"Good-by, old bunny, good-by, you're the dandiest bunny there ever was," they whispered in his long ears. And he, because he knew what they were saying and why they were saying it, he wiggled his long ears and looked long and steady at them from his deep eyes.

"Zango," they yelled. He got ready. "And now zango!" they yelled again. And the fifth jack-rabbit with his stripes and spots lifted off his feet and went on and on and on and up and up and when he came to the roof of the skyscraper he kept on going on and on and up and up till after a while he was gone all the way out of sight.

They waited and watched, they watched

and waited. He never came back. He never was heard of again. He was gone. With the stripes on his back and the spots on his hair, he was gone. And Young Leather and Red Slippers said they were glad they had kissed him on the nose before he went away on a long trip far off, so far off he never came back.

The Wooden Indian and the Shaghorn Buffalo

One night a milk white moon was shining down on Main Street. The sidewalks and the stones, the walls and the windows all stood out milk white. And there was a thin blue mist drifted and shifted like a woman's veil up and down Main Street, up to the moon and back again. Yes, all Main Street was a mist blue and a milk white, mixed up and soft all over and all through.

It was past midnight. The Wooden Indian in front of the cigar store stepped down off his stand. The Shaghorn Buffalo in front of the haberdasher shop lifted his head and shook his whiskers, raised his hoofs out of his hoof-tracks.

Then—this is what happened. They moved straight toward each other. In the middle of Main Street they met. The Wooden Indian jumped straddle of the Shaghorn Buffalo. And the Shaghorn Buffalo put his head down and ran like a prairie wind straight west on Main Street.

At the high hill over the big bend of the Clear Green River they stopped. They stood looking. Drifting and shifting like a woman's blue veil, the blue mist filled the valley and the milk white moon filled the valley. And the mist and the moon touched with a lingering, wistful kiss the clear green water of the Clear Green River.

So they stood looking, the Wooden Indian with his copper face and wooden feathers, and the Shaghorn Buffalo with his big head and

So they stood looking

heavy shoulders slumping down close to the ground.

And after they had looked a long while, and each of them got an eyeful of the high hill, the big bend and the moon mist on the river all blue and white and soft, after they had looked a long while, they turned around and the Shaghorn Buffalo put his head down and ran like a prairie wind down Main Street till he was exactly in front of the cigar store and the haberdasher shop. Then whisk! both of them were right back like they were before, standing still, taking whatever comes.

This is the story as it came from the night policeman of the Village of Cream Puffs. He told the people the next day, "I was sitting on the steps of the cigar store last night watching for burglars. And when I saw the Wooden Indian step down and the Shaghorn Buffalo step out, and the two of them go down Main Street like the wind, I says to myself, marvelish, 'tis marvelish, 'tis marvelish."

6. Four Stories About Dear, Dear Eyes

People: The White Horse Girl
The Blue Wind Boy
The Gray Man on Horseback
Six Girls With Balloons

Henry Hagglyhoagly
Susan Slackentwist
Two Wool Yarn Mittens

Peter Potato Blossom Wishes
Her Father
Many Shoes
Slippers
A Slipper Moon

The White Horse Girl and the Blue Wind Boy

When the dishes are washed at night time and the cool of the evening has come in summer or the lamps and fires are lit for the night in winter, then the fathers and mothers in the Rootabaga Country sometimes tell the young people the story of the White Horse Girl and the Blue Wind Boy.

The White Horse Girl grew up far in the west of the Rootabaga Country. All the years she grew up as a girl she liked to ride horses. Best of all things for her was to be straddle of a white horse loping with a loose bridle among the hills and along the rivers of the west Rootabaga Country.

She rode one horse white as snow, another horse white as new washed sheep wool, and another white as silver. And she could not tell because she did not know which of these three white horses she liked best.

"Snow is beautiful enough for me any time," she said, "new washed sheep wool, or silver out of a ribbon of the new moon, any or either is white enough for me. I like the white manes, the white flanks, the white noses, the white feet of all my ponies. I like the forelocks hanging down between the white ears of all three—my ponies."

And living neighbor to the White Horse Girl in the same prairie country, with the same black crows flying over their places, was the Blue Wind Boy. All the years he grew up as a boy he liked to walk with his feet in the dirt and the grass listening to the winds. Best of all things for him was to put on strong shoes and go hiking among the hills and along the rivers of the west Rootabaga Country, listening to the winds.

There was a blue wind of day time, starting sometimes six o'clock on a summer morning or eight o'clock on a winter morning. And there was a night wind with blue of summer stars in summer and blue of winter stars in winter. And there was yet another, a blue wind of the times between night and day, a blue dawn and evening wind. All three of these winds he liked so well he could not say which he liked best.

"The early morning wind is strong as the prairie and whatever I tell it I know it believes and remembers," he said, "and the night wind with the big dark curves of the night sky in it, the night wind gets inside of me and understands all my secrets. And the blue wind of the times between, in the dusk when it is neither night nor day, this is the wind that asks me

161

questions and tells me to wait and it will bring me whatever I want."

Of course, it happened as it had to happen, the White Horse Girl and the Blue Wind Boy met. She, straddling one of her white horses, and he, wearing his strong hiking shoes in the dirt and the grass, it had to happen they should meet among the hills and along the rivers of the west Rootabaga Country where they lived neighbors.

And of course, she told him all about the snow white horse and the horse white as new washed sheep wool and the horse white as a silver ribbon of the new moon. And he told her all about the blue winds he liked listening to, the early morning wind, the night sky wind, and the wind of the dusk between, the wind that asked him questions and told him to wait.

One day the two of them were gone. On the same day of the week the White Horse Girl and the Blue Wind Boy went away. And their fathers and mothers and sisters and brothers and uncles and aunts wondered about them and talked about them, because they didn't tell anybody beforehand they were going. Nobody at all knew beforehand or afterward why they were going away, the real honest why of it.

They left a short letter. It read:

To All Our Sweethearts, Old Folks and Young Folks:
We have started to go where the white horses come from and where the blue winds begin. Keep a corner in your hearts for us while we are gone.
The White Horse Girl.
The Blue Wind Boy.

That was all they had to guess by in the west Rootabaga Country, to guess and guess where two darlings had gone.

Many years passed. One day there came riding across the Rootabaga Country a Gray Man on Horseback. He looked like he had come a long ways. So they asked him the question they always asked of any rider who looked like he had come a long ways, "Did you ever see the

White Horse Girl and the Blue Wind Boy?"

"Yes," he answered, "I saw them.

"It was a long, long ways from here I saw them," he went on, "it would take years and years to ride to where they are. They were sitting together and talking to each other, sometimes singing, in a place where the land runs high and tough rocks reach up. And they were looking out across water, blue water as far as the eye could see. And away far off the blue waters met the blue sky.

" 'Look!' said the Boy, 'that's where the blue winds begin.'

"And far out on the blue waters, just a little this side of where the blue winds begin, there were white manes, white flanks, white noses, white galloping feet.

" 'Look!' said the Girl, 'that's where the white horses come from.'

"And then nearer to the land came thousands in an hour, millions in a day, white horses, some white as snow, some like new washed sheep wool, some white as silver ribbons of the new moon.

"I asked them, 'Whose place is this?' They answered, 'It belongs to us; this is what we started for; this is where the white horses come from; this is where the blue winds begin.'"

And that was all the Gray Man on Horseback would tell the people of the west Rootabaga Country. That was all he knew, he said, and if there was any more he would tell it.

And the fathers and mothers and sisters and brothers and uncles and aunts of the White Horse Girl and the Blue Wind Boy wondered and talked often about whether the Gray Man on Horseback made up the story out of his head or whether it happened just like he told it.

Anyhow this is the story they tell sometimes to the young people of the west Rootabaga Country when the dishes are washed at night and the cool of the evening has come in summer or the lamps and fires are lit for the night in winter.

What Six Girls with Balloons Told the Gray Man on Horseback

Once there came riding across the Rootabaga Country a Gray Man on Horseback. He looked as if he had come a long ways. He looked like a brother to the same Gray Man on Horseback who said he had seen the White Horse Girl and the Blue Wind Boy.

He stopped in the Village of Cream Puffs. His gray face was sad and his eyes were gray deep and sad. He spoke short and seemed strong. Sometimes his eyes looked as if they were going to flash, but instead of fire they filled with shadows.

Yet——he did laugh once. It did happen once he lifted his head and face to the sky and let loose a long ripple of laughs.

On Main Street near the Roundhouse of the Big Spool, where they wind up the string that pulls the light little town back when the wind blows it away, there he was riding slow on his gray horse when he met six girls with six fine braids of yellow hair and six balloons apiece. That is, each and every one of the six girls had six fine long braids of yellow hair and each braid of hair had a balloon tied on the end. A little blue wind was blowing and the many balloons tied to the braids of the six girls swung up and down and slow and fast whenever the blue wind went up and down and slow and fast.

For the first time since he had been in the Village, the eyes of the Gray Man filled with lights and his face began to look hopeful. He stopped his horse when he came even with the six girls and the balloons floating from the braids of yellow hair.

"Where you going?" he asked.

"Who—hoo-hoo? Who—who—who?" the six girls cheeped out.

"All six of you and your balloons, where you going?"

"Oh, hoo-hoo-hoo, back where we came from," and they all turned their heads back and forth and sideways, which of course turned all the balloons back and forth and sideways because the balloons were fastened to the fine braids of hair which were fastened to their heads.

"And where do you go when you get back where you came from?" he asked just to be asking.

"Oh, hoo-hoo-hoo, then we start out and go straight ahead and see what we can see," they all answered just to be answering and they dipped their heads and swung them up which of course dipped all the balloons and swung them up.

So they talked, he asking just to be asking

and the six balloon girls answering just to be answering.

At last his sad mouth broke into a smile and his eyes were lit like a morning sun coming up over harvest fields. And he said to them, "Tell me why are balloons—that is what I want you to tell me—why are balloons?"

The first little girl put her thumb under her chin, looked up at her six balloons floating in the little blue wind over her head, and said: "Balloons are wishes. The wind made them. The west wind makes the red balloons. The south wind makes the blue. The yellow and green balloons come from the east wind and the north wind."

The second little girl put her first finger next to her nose, looked up at her six balloons dipping up and down like hill flowers in a small wind, and said:

"A balloon used to be a flower. It got tired. Then it changed itself to a balloon. I listened one time to a yellow balloon. It was talking to itself like people talk. It said, 'I used to be a yellow pumpkin flower stuck down close to the ground, now I am a yellow balloon high up in the air where nobody can walk on me and I can see everything.' "

The third little girl held both of her ears like she was afraid they would wiggle while she slid with a skip, turned quick, and looking up at her balloons, spoke these words:

"A balloon is foam. It comes the same as soap bubbles come. A long time ago it used to be sliding along on water, river water, ocean water, waterfall water, falling and falling over a rocky waterfall, any water you want. The wind saw the bubble and picked it up and carried it away, telling it, 'Now you're a balloon—come along and see the world.' "

The fourth little girl jumped straight into the air so all six of her balloons made a jump like they were going to get loose and go to the sky—and when the little girl came down from her jump and was standing on her two feet with her head turned looking up at the six balloons, she spoke the shortest answer of all, saying:

"Balloons are to make us look up. They help our necks."

The fifth little girl stood first on one foot, then another, bent her head down to her knees and looked at her toes, then swinging straight up and looking at the flying spotted yellow and red and green balloons, she said:

"Balloons come from orchards. Look for trees where half is oranges and half is orange balloons. Look for apple trees where half is red pippins and half is red pippin balloons. Look for watermelons too. A long green balloon with white and yellow belly stripes is a ghost. It came from a watermelon said goodby."

The sixth girl, the last one, kicked the heel of her left foot with the toe of her right foot, put her thumbs under her ears and wiggled all her fingers, then stopped all her kicking and wiggling, and stood looking up at her balloons all quiet because the wind had gone down—and she murmured like she was thinking to herself:

"Balloons come from fire chasers. Every balloon has a fire chaser chasing it. All the fire chasers are made terrible quick and when they come they burn quick, so the balloon is made light so it can run away terrible quick. Balloons slip away from fire. If they don't they can't be balloons. Running away from fire keeps them light."

All the time he listened to the six girls the face of the Gray Man kept getting more hopeful. His eyes lit up. Twice he smiled. And after he said good-by and rode up the street, he lifted his head and face to the sky and let loose a long ripple of laughs.

He kept looking back when he left the Village and the last thing he saw was the six girls each with six balloons fastened to the six braids of yellow hair hanging down their backs.

The sixth little girl kicked the heel of her

173

left foot with the toe of her right foot and said, "He is a nice man. I think he must be our uncle. If he comes again we shall all ask him to tell us where he thinks balloons come from."

And the other five girls all answered, "Yes," or "Yes, yes," or "Yes, yes, yes," real fast like a balloon with a fire chaser after it.

How Henry Hagglyhoagly Played the Guitar with His Mittens On

Sometimes in January the sky comes down close if we walk on a country road, and turn our faces up to look at the sky.

Sometimes on that kind of a January night the stars look like numbers, look like the arithmetic writing of a girl going to school and just beginning arithmetic.

It was this kind of a night Henry Hagglyhoagly was walking down a country road on his way to the home of Susan Slackentwist, the daughter of the rutabaga king near the Village of Liver-and-Onions. When Henry Hagglyhoagly turned his face up to look at the sky it seemed to him as though the sky came down close to his nose, and there was a writing in stars as though some girl had been doing arithmetic examples, writing number 4 and number 7 and 4 and 7 over and over again across the sky.

"Why is it so bitter cold weather?" Henry Hagglyhoagly asked himself, "if I say many bitter bitters it is not so bitter as the cold wind and the cold weather."

"You are good, mittens, keeping my fingers warm," he said every once in a while to the wool yarn mittens on his hands.

The wind came tearing along and put its chilly, icy, clammy clamps on the nose of Henry Hagglyhoagly, fastening the clamps like a nipping, gripping clothes pin on his nose. He put his wool yarn mittens up on his nose and rubbed till the wind took off the chilly, icy, clammy

It seemed to him as though the sky came down close
to his nose

clamps. His nose was warm again; he said, "Thank you, mittens, for keeping my nose warm."

He spoke to his wool yarn mittens as though they were two kittens or pups, or two little cub bears, or two little Idaho ponies. "You're my chums keeping me company," he said to the mittens.

"Do you know what we got here under our left elbow?" he said to the mittens, "I shall mention to you what is here under my left elbow.

"It ain't a mandolin, it ain't a mouth organ nor an accordion nor a concertina nor a fiddle. It is a guitar, a Spanish Spinnish Splishy guitar made special.

"Yes, mittens, they said a strong young man like me ought to have a piano because a piano is handy to play for everybody in the house and a piano is handy to put a hat and overcoat on or books or flowers.

"I snizzled at 'em, mittens. I told 'em I

179

seen a Spanish Spinnish Splishy guitar made special in a hardware store window for eight dollars and a half.

"And so, mittens—are you listening, mittens?—after cornhusking was all husked and the oats thrashing all thrashed and the rutabaga digging all dug, I took eight dollars and a half in my inside vest pocket and I went to the hardware store.

"I put my thumbs in my vest pocket and I wiggled my fingers like a man when he is proud of what he is going to have if he gets it. And I said to the head clerk in the hardware store, 'Sir, the article I desire to purchase this evening as one of your high class customers, the article I desire to have after I buy it for myself, is the article there in the window, sir, the Spanish Spinnish Splishy guitar.'

"And, mittens, if you are listening, I am taking this Spanish Spinnish Splishy guitar to go to the home of Susan Slackentwist, the daughter of the rutabaga king near the Village of

The Guitar with His Mittens On

Liver-and-Onions, to sing a serenade song."

The cold wind of the bitter cold weather blew and blew, trying to blow the guitar out from under the left elbow of Henry Haggly-hoagly. And the worse the wind blew the tighter he held his elbow holding the guitar where he wanted it.

He walked on and on with his long legs stepping long steps till at last he stopped, held his nose in the air, and sniffed.

"Do I sniff something or do I not?" he asked, lifting his wool yarn mittens to his nose and rubbing his nose till it was warm. Again he sniffed.

"Ah hah, yeah, yeah, this is the big rutabaga field near the home of the rutabaga king and the home of his daughter, Susan Slackentwist."

At last he came to the house, stood under the window and slung the guitar around in front of him to play the music to go with the song.

"And now," he asked his mittens, "shall I take you off or keep you on? If I take you off the cold wind of the bitter cold weather will freeze my hands so stiff and bitter cold my fingers will be too stiff to play the guitar. *I will play with mittens on.*"

Which he did. He stood under the window of Susan Slackentwist and played the guitar with his mittens on, the warm wool yarn mittens he called his chums. It was the first time any strong young man going to see his sweetheart ever played the guitar with his mittens on when it was a bitter night with a cold wind and cold weather.

Susan Slackentwist opened her window and threw him a snow-bird feather to keep for a keepsake to remember her by. And for years afterward many a sweetheart in the Rootabaga Country told her lover, "If you wish to marry me let me hear you under my window on a winter night playing the guitar with wool yarn mittens on."

And when Henry Hagglyhoagly walked home on his long legs stepping long steps, he

The Guitar with His Mittens On

said to his mittens, "This Spanish Spinnish Splishy guitar made special will bring us luck." And when he turned his face up, the sky came down close and he could see stars fixed like numbers and the arithmetic writing of a girl going to school learning to write number 4 and number 7 and 4 and 7 over and over.

Never Kick a Slipper at the Moon

When a girl is growing up in the Rootabaga Country she learns some things to do, some things *not* to do.

"Never kick a slipper at the moon if it is the time for the Dancing Slipper Moon when the slim early moon looks like the toe and the heel of a dancer's foot," was the advice Mr. Wishes, the father of Peter Potato Blossom Wishes, gave to his daughter.

"Why?" she asked him.

"Because your slipper will go straight up, on and on to the moon, and fasten itself on the moon as if the moon is a foot ready for dancing," said Mr. Wishes.

185

Never Kick a Slipper at the Moon

"A long time ago there was one night when a secret word was passed around to all the shoes standing in the bedrooms and closets.

"The whisper of the secret was: 'To-night all the shoes and the slippers and the boots of the world are going walking without any feet in them. To-night when those who put us on their feet in the daytime, are sleeping in their beds, we all get up and walk and go walking where we walk in the daytime.'

"And in the middle of the night, when the people in the beds were sleeping, the shoes and the slippers and the boots everywhere walked out of the bedrooms and the closets. Along the sidewalks on the streets, up and down stairways, along hallways, the shoes and slippers and the boots tramped and marched and stumbled.

"Some walked pussyfoot, sliding easy and soft just like people in the daytime. Some walked clumping and clumping, coming down heavy on the heels and slow on the toes, just like people in the daytime.

"Some turned their toes in and walked pigeon-toe, some spread their toes out and held their heels in, just like people in the daytime. Some ran glad and fast, some lagged slow and sorry.

"Now there was a little girl in the Village of Cream Puffs who came home from a dance that night. And she was tired from dancing round dances and square dances, one steps and two steps, toe dances and toe and heel dances, dances close up and dances far apart, she was so tired she took off only one slipper, tumbled onto her bed and went to sleep with one slipper on.

"She woke up in the morning when it was yet dark. And she went to the window and looked up in the sky and saw a Dancing Slipper Moon dancing far and high in the deep blue sea of the moon sky.

" 'Oh—what a moon—what a dancing slipper of a moon!' she cried with a little song to herself.

"She opened the window, saying again, 'Oh! what a moon!'—and kicked her foot with the slipper on it straight toward the moon.

"The slipper flew off and flew up and went on and on and up and up in the moonshine.

"It never came back, that slipper. It was never seen again. When they asked the girl about it she said, 'It slipped off my foot and went up and up and the last I saw of it the slipper was going on straight to the moon.' "

And these are the explanations why fathers and mothers in the Rootabaga Country say to their girls growing up, "Never kick a slipper at the moon if it is the time of the Dancing Slipper Moon when the ends of the moon look like the toe and the heel of a dancer's foot."

7. One Story — "Only the Fire-Born Understand Blue"

People: Fire the Goat
Flim the Goose
Shadows

Sand Flat Shadows

Fire the Goat and Flim the Goose slept out. Stub pines stood over them. And away up next over the stub pines were stars.

It was a white sand flat they slept on. The floor of the sand flat ran straight to the Big Lake of the Booming Rollers.

And just over the sand flat and just over the booming rollers was a high room where the mist people were making pictures. Gray pictures, blue and sometimes a little gold, and often silver, were the pictures.

And next just over the high room where the mist people were making pictures, next just over were the stars.

Over everything and always last and highest of all, were the stars.

Fire the Goat took off his horns. Flim the Goose took off his wings. "This is where we sleep," they said to each other, "here in the stub pines on the sand flats next to the booming rollers and high over everything and always last and highest of all, the stars."

Fire the Goat laid his horns under his head. Flim the Goose laid his wings under his head. "This is the best place for what you want to keep," they said to each other. Then they crossed their fingers for luck and lay down and went to sleep and slept. And while they slept the mist people went on making pictures. Gray pictures, blue and sometimes a little gold but more often silver, such were the pictures the mist people went on making while Fire the Goat and Flim the Goose went on sleeping. And over everything and always last and highest of all, were the stars.

They woke up. Fire the Goat took his horns

out and put them on. "It's morning now," he said.

Flim the Goose took his wings out and put them on. "It's another day now," he said.

Then they sat looking. Away off where the sun was coming up, inching and pushing up far across the rim curve of the Big Lake of the Booming Rollers, along the whole line of the east sky, there were people and animals, all black or all so gray they were near black.

There was a big horse with his mouth open, ears laid back, front legs thrown in two curves like harvest sickles.

There was a camel with two humps, moving slow and grand like he had all the time of all the years of all the world to go in.

There was an elephant without any head, with six short legs. There were many cows. There was a man with a club over his shoulder and a woman with a bundle on the back of her neck.

And they marched on. They were going

nowhere, it seemed. And they were going slow. They had plenty of time. There was nothing else to do. It was fixed for them to do it, long ago it was fixed. And so they were marching.

Sometimes the big horse's head sagged and dropped off and came back again. Sometimes the humps of the camel sagged and dropped off and came back again. And sometimes the club on the man's shoulder got bigger and heavier and the man staggered under it and then his legs got bigger and stronger and he steadied himself and went on. And again sometimes the bundle on the back of the neck of the woman got bigger and heavier and the bundle sagged and the woman staggered and her legs got bigger and stronger and she steadied herself and went on.

This was the show, the hippodrome, the spectacular circus that passed on the east sky before the eyes of Fire the Goat and Flim the Goose.

"Which is this, who are they and why do

Away off where the sun was coming up, there were
people and animals

they come?" Flim the Goose asked Fire the Goat.

"Do you ask me because you wish me to tell you?" asked Fire the Goat.

"Indeed it is a question to which I want an honest answer."

"Has never the father or mother nor the uncle or aunt nor the kith and kin of Flim the Goose told him the what and the which of this?"

"Never has the such of this which been put here this way to me by anybody."

Flim the Goose held up his fingers and said, "I don't talk to you with my fingers crossed."

And so Fire the Goat began to explain to Flim the Goose all about the show, the hippodrome, the mastodonic cyclopean spectacle which was passing on the east sky in front of the sun coming up.

"People say they are shadows," began Fire the Goat. "That is a name, a word, a little cough and a couple of syllables.

"For some people shadows are comic and only to laugh at. For some other people shadows are like a mouth and its breath. The breath comes out and it is nothing. It is like air and nobody can make it into a package and carry it away. It will not melt like gold nor can you shovel it like cinders. So to these people it means nothing.

"And then there are other people," Fire the Goat went on. "There are other people who understand shadows. The fire-born understand. The fire-born know where shadows come from and why they are.

"Long ago, when the Makers of the World were done making the round earth, the time came when they were ready to make the animals to put on the earth. They were not sure how to make the animals. They did not know what shape animals they wanted.

"And so they practised. They did not make real animals at first. They made only shapes of animals. And these shapes were shadows,

shadows like these you and I, Fire the Goat and Flim the Goose, are looking at this morning across the booming rollers on the east sky where the sun is coming up.

"The shadow horse over there on the east sky with his mouth open, his ears laid back, and his front legs thrown in a curve like harvest sickles, that shadow horse was one they made long ago when they were practising to make a real horse. That shadow horse was a mistake and they threw him away. Never will you see two shadow horses alike. All shadow horses on the sky are different. Each one is a mistake, a shadow horse thrown away because he was not good enough to be a real horse.

"That elephant with no head on his neck, stumbling so grand on six legs—and that grand camel with two humps, one bigger than the other—and those cows with horns in front and behind—they are all mistakes, they were all thrown away because they were not made good enough to be real elephants, real cows, real

199

camels. They were made just for practice, away back early in the world before any real animals came on their legs to eat and live and be here like the rest of us.

"That man—see him now staggering along with the club over his shoulder—see how his long arms come to his knees and sometimes his hands drag below his feet. See how heavy the club on his shoulders loads him down and drags him on. He is one of the oldest shadow men. He was a mistake and they threw him away. He was made just for practice.

"And that woman. See her now at the end of that procession across the booming rollers on the east sky. See her the last of all, the end of the procession. On the back of her neck a bundle. Sometimes the bundle gets bigger. The woman staggers. Her legs get bigger and stronger. She picks herself up and goes along shaking her head. She is the same as the others. She is a shadow and she was made as a mistake.

200

Early, early in the beginnings of the world she was made, for practice.

"Listen, Flim the Goose. What I am telling you is a secret of the fire-born. I do not know whether you understand. We have slept together a night on the sand flats next to the booming rollers, under the stub pines with the stars high over—and so I tell what the fathers of the fire-born tell their sons."

And that day Fire the Goat and Flim the Goose moved along the sand flat shore of the Big Lake of the Booming Rollers. It was a blue day, with a fire-blue of the sun mixing itself in the air and the water. Off to the north the booming rollers were blue sea-green. To the east they were sometimes streak purple, sometimes changing bluebell stripes. And to the south they were silver blue, sheet blue.

Where the shadow hippodrome marched on the east sky that morning was a long line of blue-bird spots.

"Only the fire-born understand blue," said Fire the Goat to Flim the Goose. And that night as the night before they slept on a sand flat. And again Fire the Goat took off his horns and laid them under his head while he slept and Flim the Goose took off his wings and laid them under his head while he slept.

And twice in the night, Fire the Goat whispered in his sleep, whispered to the stars, "Only the fire-born understand blue."

8. Two Stories About Corn Fairies,
    Blue Foxes, Flongboos and Hap-
    penings That Happened in the
    United States and Canada

> *People:* Spink
>   Skabootch
>   A Man
>   Corn Fairies
>
>   Blue Foxes
>   Flongboos
>   A Philadelphia Policeman
>   Passenger Conductor
>   Chicago Newspapers
>   The Head Spotter of the
>   Weather Makers at Medi-
>   cine Hat

How to Tell Corn Fairies If You See 'Em

If you have ever watched the little corn begin to march across the black lands and then slowly change to big corn and go marching on from the little corn moon of summer to the big corn harvest moon of autumn, then you must have guessed who it is that helps the corn come along. It is the corn fairies. Leave out the corn fairies and there wouldn't be any corn.

All children know this. All boys and girls know that corn is no good unless there are corn fairies.

Have you ever stood in Illinois or Iowa and

watched the late summer wind or the early fall wind running across a big cornfield? It looks as if a big, long blanket were being spread out for dancers to come and dance on. If you look close and if you listen close you can see the corn fairies come dancing and singing—sometimes. If it is a wild day and a hot sun is pouring down while a cool north wind blows—and this happens sometimes—then you will be sure to see thousands of corn fairies marching and countermarching in mocking grand marches over the big, long blanket of green and silver. Then too they sing, only you must listen with your littlest and newest ears if you wish to hear their singing. They sing soft songs that go pla-sizzy pla-sizzy-sizzy, and each song is softer than an eye wink, softer than a Nebraska baby's thumb.

And Spink, who is a little girl living in the same house with the man writing this story, and Skabootch, who is another little girl in the same house—both Spink and Skabootch are asking the question, "How can we tell corn fairies if

we see 'em? If we meet a corn fairy how will
we know it?" And this is the explanation the
man gave to Spink who is older than Skabootch,
and to Skabootch who is younger than Spink:—

All corn fairies wear overalls. They work
hard, the corn fairies, and they are proud. The
reason they are proud is because they work so
hard. And the reason they work so hard is because they have overalls.

But understand this. The overalls are corn
gold cloth, woven from leaves of ripe corn
mixed with ripe October corn silk. In the first
week of the harvest moon coming up red and
changing to yellow and silver the corn fairies
sit by thousands between the corn rows weaving
and stitching the clothes they have to wear
next winter, next spring, next summer.

They sit cross-legged when they sew. And it
is a law among them each one must point the
big toe at the moon while sewing the harvest
moon clothes. When the moon comes up red
as blood early in the evening they point their

big toes slanting toward the east. Then to-wards midnight when the moon is yellow and half way up the sky their big toes are only half slanted as they sit cross-legged sewing. And after midnight when the moon sails its silver disk high overhead and toward the west, then the corn fairies sit sewing with their big toes pointed nearly straight up.

If it is a cool night and looks like frost, then the laughter of the corn fairies is something worth seeing. All the time they sit sewing their next year clothes they are laughing. It is not a law they have to laugh. They laugh because they are half-tickled and glad because it is a good corn year.

And whenever the corn fairies laugh then the laugh comes out of the mouth like a thin gold frost. If you should be lucky enough to see a thousand corn fairies sitting between the corn rows and all of them laughing, you would laugh with wonder yourself to see the gold frost coming from their mouths while they laughed.

If You See 'Em

Travelers who have traveled far, and seen many things, say that if you know the corn fairies with a real knowledge you can always tell by the stitches in their clothes what state they are from.

In Illinois the corn fairies stitch fifteen stitches of ripe corn silk across the woven corn leaf cloth. In Iowa they stitch sixteen stitches, in Nebraska seventeen, and the farther west you go the more corn silk stitches the corn fairies have in the corn cloth clothes they wear.

In Minnesota one year there were fairies with a blue sash of corn-flowers across the breast. In the Dakotas the same year all the fairies wore pumpkin-flower neckties, yellow four-in-hands and yellow ascots. And in one strange year it happened in both the states of Ohio and Texas the corn fairies wore little wristlets of white morning glories.

The traveler who heard about this asked many questions and found out the reason why that year the corn fairies wore little wristlets of white morning glories. He said, "Whenever fairies are sad they wear white. And this year, which was long ago, was the year men were tearing down all the old zigzag rail fences. Now those old zigzag rail fences were beautiful for the fairies because a hundred fairies could sit on one rail and thousands and thousands of them could sit on the zigzags and sing pla-sizzy pla-sizzy, softer than an eye-wink, softer than a baby's thumb, all on a moonlight summer night. And they found out that year was going to be the last year of the zigzag rail fences. It made them sorry and sad, and when they are sorry and sad they wear white. So they picked the wonderful white morning glories running along the zigzag rail fences and made them into little wristlets and wore those wristlets the next year to show they were sorry and sad."

Of course, all this helps you to know how the corn fairies look in the evening, the night

time and the moonlight.   Now we shall see
how they look in the day time.

In the day time the corn fairies have their
overalls of corn gold cloth on.   And they walk
among the corn rows and climb the corn stalks
and fix things in the leaves and stalks and ears
of the corn.   They help it to grow.

Each one carries on the left shoulder a mouse
brush to brush away the field mice.   And over
the right shoulder each one has a cricket broom
to sweep away the crickets.   The brush is a
whisk brush to brush away mice that get foolish.
And the broom is to sweep away crickets that
get foolish.

Around the middle of each corn fairy is a yellow-belly belt.   And stuck in this belt is a purple moon shaft hammer.   Whenever the wind
blows strong and nearly blows the corn down,
then the fairies run out and take their purple
moon shaft hammers out of their yellow-belly
belts and nail down nails to keep the corn from

blowing down. When a rain storm is blowing up terrible and driving all kinds of terribles across the cornfield, then you can be sure of one thing. Running like the wind among the corn rows are the fairies, jerking their purple moon shaft hammers out of their belts and nailing nails down to keep the corn standing up so it will grow and be ripe and beautiful when the harvest moon comes again in the fall.

Spink and Skabootch ask where the corn fairies get the nails. The answer to Spink and Skabootch is, "Next week you will learn all about where the corn fairies get the nails to nail down the corn if you will keep your faces washed and your ears washed till next week."

And the next time you stand watching a big cornfield in late summer or early fall, when the wind is running across the green and silver, listen with your littlest and newest ears. Maybe you will hear the corn fairies going pla-sizzy pla-sizzy-sizzy, softer than an eye wink, softer than a Nebraska baby's thumb.

How the Animals Lost Their Tails and Got Them Back Traveling From Philadelphia to Medicine Hat

Far up in North America, near the Saskatchewan river, in the Winnipeg wheat country, not so far from the town of Moose Jaw named for the jaw of a moose shot by a hunter there, up where the blizzards and the chinooks begin, where nobody works unless they have to and they nearly all have to, there stands the place known as Medicine Hat.

And there on a high stool in a high tower

213

on a high hill sits the Head Spotter of the Weather Makers.

When the animals lost their tails it was because the Head Spotter of the Weather Makers at Medicine Hat was careless.

The tails of the animals were stiff and dry because for a long while there was dusty dry weather. Then at last came rain. And the water from the sky poured on the tails of the animals and softened them.

Then the chilly chills came whistling with icy mittens and they froze all the tails stiff. A big wind blew up and blew and blew till all the tails of the animals blew off.

It was easy for the fat stub hogs with their fat stub tails. But it was not so easy for the blue fox who uses his tail to help him when he runs, when he eats, when he walks or talks, when he makes pictures or writes letters in the snow or when he puts a snack of bacon meat with stripes of fat and lean to hide till he wants it under a big rock by a river.

There on a high stool in a high tower, on a high hill
sits the Head Spotter of the Weather Makers

It was easy enough for the rabbit who has long ears and no tail at all except a white thumb of cotton. But it was hard for the yellow flongboo who at night lights up his house in a hollow tree with his fire yellow torch of a tail. It is hard for the yellow flongboo to lose his tail because it lights up his way when he sneaks at night on the prairie, sneaking up on the flangwayers, the hippers and hangjasts, so good to eat.

The animals picked a committee of representatives to represent them in a parleyhoo to see what steps could be taken by talking to do something. There were sixty-six representatives on the committee and they decided to call it the Committee of Sixty Six. It was a distinguished committee and when they all sat together holding their mouths under their noses (just like a distinguished committee) and blinking their eyes up over their noses and cleaning their ears and scratching themselves under the chin looking thoughtful (just like a distinguished committee) then anybody would say just to look at them, "This must be quite a distinguished committee."

Of course, they would all have looked more distinguished if they had had their tails on. If the big wavy streak of a blue tail blows off behind a blue fox, he doesn't look near so distinguished. Or, if the long yellow torch of a tail blows off behind a yellow flongboo, he doesn't look so distinguished as he did before the wind blew.

So the Committee of Sixty Six had a meeting and a parleyhoo to decide what steps could be taken by talking to do something. For chairman they picked an old flongboo who was an umpire and used to umpire many mix-ups. Among the flongboos he was called "the umpire of umpires," "the king of umpires," "the prince of umpires," "the peer of umpires." When there was a fight and a snag and a wrangle between two families living next door neighbors to each other and this old flongboo

218

was called in to umpire and to say which family
was right and which family was wrong, which
family started it and which family ought to
stop it, he used to say, "The best umpire is the
one who knows just how far to go and how far
not to go." He was from Massachusetts, born
near Chappaquiddick, this old flongboo, and he
lived there in a horse chestnut tree six feet thick
half way between South Hadley and North-
ampton. And at night, before he lost his tail,
he lighted up the big hollow cave inside the
horse chestnut tree with his yellow torch of a
tail.

After he was nominated with speeches and
elected with votes to be the chairman, he stood
up on the platform and took a gavel and banged
with the gavel and made the Committee of
Sixty Six come to order.

"It is no picnic to lose your tail and we are
here for business," he said, banging his gavel
again.

A blue fox from Waco, Texas, with his ears

full of dry bluebonnet leaves from a hole where he lived near the Brazos river, stood up and said, "Mr. Chairman, do I have the floor?"

"You have whatever you get away with—I get your number," said the chairman.

"I make a motion," said the blue fox from Waco, "and I move you, Sir, that this committee get on a train at Philadelphia and ride on the train till it stops and then take another train and take more trains and keep on riding till we get to Medicine Hat, near the Saskatchewan river, in the Winnipeg wheat country where the Head Spotter of the Weather Makers sits on a high stool in a high tower on a high hill spotting the weather. There we will ask him if he will respectfully let us beseech him to bring back weather that will bring back our tails. It was the weather took away our tails; it is the weather can bring back our tails."

"All in favor of the motion," said the chairman, "will clean their right ears with their right paws."

And all the blue foxes and all the yellow flongboos began cleaning their right ears with their right paws.

"All who are against the motion will clean their left ears with their left paws," said the chairman.

And all the blue foxes and all the yellow flongboos began cleaning their left ears with their left paws.

"The motion is carried both ways—it is a razmataz," said the chairman. "Once again, all in favor of the motion will stand up on the toes of their hind legs and stick their noses straight up in the air." And all the blue foxes and all the yellow flongboos stood up on the toes of their hind legs and stuck their noses straight up in the air.

"And now," said the chairman, "all who are against the motion will stand on the top and the apex of their heads, stick their hind legs straight up in the air, and make a noise like a woof woof."

And then not one of the blue foxes and not one of the yellow flongboos stood on the top and the apex of his head nor stuck his hind legs up in the air nor made a noise like a woof woof.

"The motion is carried and this is no picnic," said the chairman.

So the committee went to Philadelphia to get on a train to ride on.

"Would you be so kind as to tell us the way to the union depot," the chairman asked a policeman. It was the first time a flongboo ever spoke to a policeman on the streets of Philadelphia.

"It pays to be polite," said the policeman.

"May I ask you again if you would kindly direct us to the union depot? We wish to ride on a train," said the flongboo.

"Polite persons and angry persons are different kinds," said the policeman.

The flongboo's eyes changed their lights and a slow torch of fire sprang out behind where his tail used to be. And speaking to the policeman, he said, "Sir, I must inform you, publicly and respectfully, that we are The Committee of Sixty Six. We are honorable and distinguished representatives from places your honest and ignorant geography never told you about. This committee is going to ride on the cars to Medicine Hat near the Saskatchewan river in the Winnipeg wheat country where the blizzards and chinooks begin. We have a special message and a secret errand for the Head Spotter of the Weather Makers."

"I am a polite friend of all respectable people —that is why I wear this star to arrest people who are not respectable," said the policeman, touching with his pointing finger the silver and nickel star fastened with a safety pin on his blue uniform coat.

"This is the first time ever in the history of the United States that a committee of sixty-six blue foxes and flongboos has ever visited a city in the United States," insinuated the flongboo.

"I beg to be mistaken," finished the policeman. "The union depot is under that clock." And he pointed to a clock near by.

"I thank you for myself, I thank you for the Committee of Sixty Six, I thank you for the sake of all the animals in the United States who have lost their tails," finished the chairman.

Over to the Philadelphia union depot they went, all sixty-six, half blue foxes, half flongboos. As they pattered pitty-pat, pitty-pat, each with feet and toenails, ears and hair, everything but tails, into the Philadelphia union depot, they had nothing to say. And yet though they had nothing to say the passengers in the union depot waiting for trains thought they had something to say and were saying it. So the passengers in the union depot waiting for trains listened. But with all their listening the passengers never heard the blue foxes and yellow flongboos say anything.

"They are saying it to each other in some

224

strange language from where they belong," said one passenger waiting for a train.

"They have secrets to keep among each other, and never tell us," said another passenger.

"We will find out all about it reading the newspapers upside down to-morrow morning," said a third passenger.

Then the blue foxes and the yellow flongboos pattered pitty-pat, pitty-pat, each with feet and toenails, ears and hair, everything except tails, pattered scritch scratch over the stone floors out into the train shed. They climbed into a special smoking car hooked on ahead of the engine.

"This car hooked on ahead of the engine was put on special for us so we will always be ahead and we will get there before the train does," said the chairman to the committee.

The train ran out of the train shed. It kept on the tracks and never left the rails. It came to the Horseshoe Curve near Altoona where the tracks bend like a big horseshoe. Instead of going around the long winding bend of the horseshoe tracks up and around the mountains, the train acted different. The train jumped off the tracks down into the valley and cut across in a straight line on a cut-off, jumped on the tracks again and went on toward Ohio.

The conductor said, "If you are going to jump the train off the tracks, tell us about it beforehand."

"When we lost our tails nobody told us about it beforehand," said the old flongboo umpire.

Two baby blue foxes, the youngest on the committee, sat on the front platform. Mile after mile of chimneys went by. Four hundred smokestacks stood in a row and tubs on tubs of sooty black soot marched out.

"This is the place where the black cats come to be washed," said the first baby blue fox.

"I believe your affidavit," said the second blue fox.

Crossing Ohio and Indiana at night the flongboos took off the roof of the car. The conductor told them, "I must have an explanation." "It was between us and the stars," they told him.

The train ran into Chicago. That afternoon there were pictures upside down in the newspapers showing the blue foxes and the yellow flongboos climbing telephone poles standing on their heads eating pink ice cream with iron axes.

Each blue fox and yellow flongboo got a newspaper for himself and each one looked long and careful upside down to see how he looked in the picture in the newspaper climbing a telephone pole standing on his head eating pink ice cream with an iron ax.

Crossing Minnesota the sky began to fill with the snow ghosts of Minnesota snow weather. Again the foxes and flongboos lifted the roof off the car, telling the conductor they would rather wreck the train than miss the big show of the snow ghosts of the first Minnesota snow weather of the winter.

Some went to sleep but the two baby blue foxes stayed up all night watching the snow ghosts and telling snow ghost stories to each other.

Early in the night the first baby blue fox said to the second, "Who are the snow ghosts the ghosts of?" The second baby blue fox answered, "Everybody who makes a snowball, a snow man, a snow fox or a snow fish or a snow pattycake, everybody has a snow ghost."

And that was only the beginning of their talk. It would take a big book to tell all that the two baby foxes told each other that night about the Minnesota snow ghosts, because they sat up all night telling old stories their fathers and mothers and grandfathers and grandmothers told them, and making up new stories never heard before about where the snow ghosts go on Christmas morning and how the snow ghosts watch the New Year in.

Tails and Got Them Back

Somewhere between Winnipeg and Moose Jaw, somewhere it was they stopped the train and all ran out in the snow where the white moon was shining down a valley of birch trees. It was the Snowbird Valley where all the snowbirds of Canada come early in the winter and make their snow shoes.

At last they came to Medicine Hat, near the Saskatchewan River, where the blizzards and the chinooks begin, where nobody works unless they have to and they nearly all have to. There they ran in the snow till they came to the place where the Head Spotter of the Weather Makers sits on a high stool in a high tower on a high hill watching the weather.

"Let loose another big wind to blow back our tails to us, let loose a big freeze to freeze our tails onto us again, and so let us get back our lost tails," they said to the Head Spotter of the Weather Makers.

Which was just what he did, giving them exactly what they wanted, so they all went back home satisfied, the blue foxes each with a big wavy brush of a tail to help him when he runs, when he eats, when he walks or talks, when he makes pictures or writes letters in the snow or when he puts a snack of bacon meat with stripes of fat and lean to hide till he wants it under a big rock by the river—and the yellow flongboos each with a long yellow torch of a tail to light up his home in a hollow tree or to light up his way when he sneaks at night on the prairie, sneaking up on the flangwayer, the hipper or the hangjast.

ROOTABAGA PIGEONS

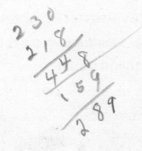

To Three Illinois Pigeons

1. Two Stories Told by the Potato Face Blind Man.

People: Blixie Bimber
Blixie Bimber's Mother
The Potato Face Blind Man
A Green Rat with the Rheumatism
Bricklayers
Mortar Men
Riveters
A Skyscraper

Slipfoot
A Stairway to the Moon
A Trapeze

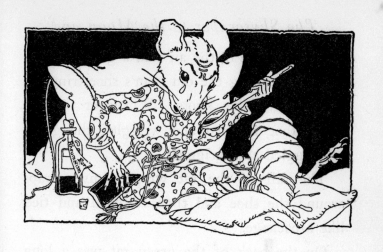

The Skyscraper to the Moon and How the Green Rat with the Rheumatism Ran a Thousand Miles Twice

Blixie Bimber's mother was chopping hash. And the hatchet broke. So Blixie started downtown with fifteen cents to buy a new hash hatchet for chopping hash.

Downtown she peeped around the corner next nearest the postoffice where the Potato Face Blind Man sat with his accordion. And the old man had his legs crossed, one foot on the sidewalk, the other foot up in the air.

3

The foot up in the air had a green rat sitting on it, tying the old man's shoestrings in knots and double knots. Whenever the old man's foot wiggled and wriggled the green rat wiggled and wriggled.

The tail of the rat wrapped five wraps around the shoe and then fastened and tied like a package.

On the back of the green rat was a long white swipe from the end of the nose to the end of the tail. Two little white swipes stuck up over the eyelashes. And five short thick swipes of white played pussy-wants-a-corner back of the ears and along the ribs of the green rat.

They were talking, the old man and the green rat, talking about alligators and why the alligators keep their baby shoes locked up in trunks over the winter time—and why the rats in the moon lock their mittens in ice boxes.

"I had the rheumatism last summer a year

4

ago," said the rat. "I had the rheumatism so bad I ran a thousand miles south and west till I came to the Egg Towns and stopped in the Village of Eggs Up."

"So?" quizzed the Potato Face.

"There in the Village of Eggs Up, they asked me, 'Do you know how to stop the moon moving?' I answered them, 'Yes, I know how—a baby alligator told me—but I told the baby alligator I wouldn't tell.'

"Many years ago there in that Village of Eggs Up they started making a skyscraper to go up till it reached the moon. They said, 'We will step in the elevator and go up to the roof and sit on the roof and eat supper on the moon.'

"The bricklayers and the mortar men and the iron riveters and the wheelbarrowers and the plasterers went higher and higher making that skyscraper, till at last they were half way up to the moon, saying to each other while they

5

worked, 'We will step in the elevator and go up to the roof and sit on the roof and eat supper on the moon.'

"Yes, they were halfway up to the moon. And that night looking at the moon they saw it move and they said to each other, 'We must stop the moon moving,' and they said later, 'We don't know how to stop the moon moving.'

"And the bricklayers and the mortar men and the iron riveters and the wheelbarrowers and the plasterers said to each other, 'If we go on now and make this skyscraper it will miss the moon and we will never go up in the elevator and sit on the roof and eat supper on the moon.'

"So they took the skyscraper down and started making it over again, aiming it straight at the moon again. And one night standing looking at the moon they saw it move and they said to each other, 'We must stop the moon moving,' saying later to each other, 'We don't know how to stop the moon moving.'

"And now they stand in the streets at night there in the Village of Eggs Up, stretching their necks looking at the moon, and asking each other, 'Why does the moon move and how can we stop the moon moving?'

"Whenever I saw them standing there stretching their necks looking at the moon, I had a zig-zag ache in my left hind foot and I wanted to tell them what the baby alligator told me, the secret of how to stop the moon moving. One night that ache zig-zagged me so—way inside my left hind foot—it zig-zagged so I ran home here a thousand miles."

The Potato Face Blind Man wriggled his shoe—and the green rat wriggled—and the long white swipe from the end of the nose to the end of the tail of the green rat wriggled.

"Is your rheumatism better?" the old man asked.

The rat answered, "Any rheumatism is better if you run a thousand miles twice."

7

The Skyscraper to the Moon

And Blixie Bimber going home with the fifteen cent hash hatchet for her mother to chop hash, Blixie said to herself, "It is a large morning to be thoughtful about."

Slipfoot and How He Nearly Always Never Gets What He Goes After

Blixie Bimber flipped out of the kitchen one morning, first saying good-by to the dish-pan, good-by to the dish-rag, good-by to the dish-towel for wiping dishes.

Under one arm she put a basket of peonies she picked, under the other arm she put a basket of jonquils she picked.

Then she flipped away up the street and downtown where she put the baskets of peonies

9

and jonquils one on each side of the Potato Face Blind Man.

"I picked the pink and lavender peonies and I picked the yellow jonquils for you to be smelling one on each side of you this fine early summer morning," she said to the Potato Face. "Have you seen anybody good to see lately?"

"Slipfoot was here this morning," said the old man.

"And who is Slipfoot?" asked Blixie.

"I don't know. He says to me, 'I got a foot always slips. I used to wash windows—and my foot slips. I used to be king of the collar buttons, king of a million dollars—and my foot slips. I used to be king of the peanuts, king of a million dollars again. I used to be king of the oyster cans, selling a million cans a day. I used to be king of the peanut sacks, selling ten million sacks a day. And every time I was a king my foot slips. Every time I had a million dollars my foot slips. Every

On the last step of the stairway my foot slips

time I went high and put my foot higher my foot slips. Somebody gave me a slipfoot. I always slip.' "

"So you call him Slipfoot?" asked Blixie.

"Yes," said the old man.

"Has he been here before?"

"Yes, he was here a year ago, saying, 'I marry a woman and she runs away. I run after her—and my foot slips. I always get what I want—and then my foot slips.

"I ran up a stairway to the moon one night. I shoveled a big sack full of little gold beans, little gold bricks, little gold bugs, on the moon and I ran down the stairway from the moon. On the last step of the stairway, my foot slips —and all the little gold beans, all the little gold bricks, all the little gold bugs, spill out and spill away. When I get down the stairway I am holding the sack and the sack holds nothing. I am all right always till my foot slips.

"I jump on a trapeze and I go swinging,

13

swinging, swinging out where I am going to take hold of the rainbow and bring it down where we can look at it close. And I hang by my feet on the trapeze and I am swinging out where I am just ready to take hold of the rainbow and bring it down. Then my foot slips."

"What is the matter with Slipfoot?" asks Blixie.

"He asks me that same question," answered the Potato Face Blind Man. "He asks me that every time he comes here. I tell him all he needs is to get his slipfoot fixed so it won't slip. Then he'll be all right."

"I understand you," said Blixie. "You make it easy. You always make it easy. And before I run away will you promise me to smell of the pink and lavender peonies and the yellow jonquils all day to-day?"

"I promise," said the Potato Face. "Promises are easy. I like promises."

"So do I," said the little girl. "It's prom-

14

ises pushing me back home to the dish-pan, the dish-rag, and the dish-towel for wiping dishes."

"Look out you don't get a slipfoot," warned the old man as the girl flipped up the street going home.

15

2. Two Stories About Bugs and Eggs.

People: Little Bugs
Big Bugs
The Rag Doll
The Broom Handle
Hammer and Nails
The Hot Cookie Pan
The Ice Tongs
The Coal Bucket
The Bushel Basket
Jack Knife
Kindling Wood
Splinters

Shush Shush
The Postmaster
The Hardware Man
The Policeman
The Postmaster's Hat
A Buff Banty Egg

Many, Many Weddings in One Corner House

There was a corner house with corners every way it looked. And up in the corners were bugs with little bug houses, bug doors to open, bug windows to look out of.

In the summer time if the evening was cool or in the winter time if the evening was warm, they played games—bugs-up, bugs-down, run-bugs-run, beans-bugs-beans.

This corner house was the place the Rag

Doll and the Broom Handle came to after their wedding. This was the same time those old people, Hammer and Nails, moved into the corner house with all the little Hammers and all the little Nails.

So there they were, the young couple, the Rag Doll and the Broom Handle, and that old family, Hammer and Nails, and up in the corners among the eave troughs and the roof shingles, the bugs with little bug houses, bug doors to open, bug windows to look out of, and bug games—bugs-up, bugs-down, run-bugs-run, or beans-bugs-beans.

Around the corner of the house every Saturday morning came the Hot Cookie Pan with a pan of hot cookies for Sunday, Monday, Tuesday, Wednesday and the rest of the week.

The Ice Tongs came with ice, the Coal Bucket came with coal, the Potato Sack came with potatoes. And the Bushel Basket was always going or coming and saying under his breath, *"Bushels, bushels, bushels."*

20

The Hot Cookie Pan came with a pan of hot cookies
and the Coal Bucket with coal

In One Corner House

One day the bugs in the little bug houses opened the bug doors and looked out of the bug windows and said to each other, "They are washing their shirts and sewing on buttons— there is going to be a wedding."

And the next day the bugs said, "They are going to have a wedding and a wedding breakfast for Jack Knife and Kindling Wood. They are asking everybody in the kitchen, the cellar, and the back yard, to come."

The wedding day came. The people came. From all over the kitchen, the cellar, the back yard, they came. The Rag Doll and the Broom Handle were there. Hammer and Nails and all the little Hammers and all the little Nails were there. The Ice Tongs, the Coal Bucket, the Potato Sack, were all there —and the Bushel Basket going and coming and saying under his breath, *"Bushels, bushels, bushels."* And, of course, the Hot Cookie Pan was there hopping up and down with hot cookies.

Many, Many Weddings

So Jack Knife and Kindling Wood began living in the corner house. A child came. They named her Splinters. And the Hot Cookie Pan and Splinters met and kissed each other and sat together in cozy corners close to each other.

And the bugs high up in the corners in the little bug houses, they opened the bug doors, looked out of the bug windows and said, "They are washing their shirts and sewing on buttons, there is a wedding again—the Hot Cookie Pan and Splinters."

And now they have many, many children, the Hot Cookie Pan and Splinters. Their children have gone all over the world and everybody knows them.

"Whenever you find a splinter or a sliver or a shiny little shaving of wood in a hot cookie," the bugs in the little bug houses say, "whenever you find a splinter or a sliver or a shiny little shaving of wood in a hot cookie, it is the child of the Hot Cookie Pan and the girl named Splinters, the daughter of Jack Knife and Kindling Wood, who grew up and married the Hot Cookie Pan."

And sometimes if a little bug asks a big bug a queer, quivvical, quizzical question hard to answer, the big bug opens a bug door, looks out of a bug window and says to the little bug, "If you don't believe what we tell you, go and ask Hammer and Nails or any of the little Hammers and Nails. Then run and listen to the Bushel Basket going and coming and saying under his breath, *'Bushels, bushels, bushels.'*"

Shush Shush, the Big Buff Banty Hen Who Laid an Egg in the Postmaster's Hat

Shush Shush was a big buff banty hen. She lived in a coop. Sometimes she marched out of the coop and went away and laid eggs. But always she came back to the coop.

And whenever she went to the front door and laid an egg in the door-bell, she rang the bell once for one egg, twice for two eggs, and a dozen rings for a dozen eggs.

Once Shush Shush went into the house of the Sniggers family and laid an egg in the piano. Another time she climbed up in the clock and laid an egg in the clock. But always she came back to the coop.

One summer morning Shush Shush marched out through the front gate, up to the next corner and the next, till she came to the post-office. There she walked into the office of the postmaster and laid an egg in the postmaster's hat.

The postmaster put on his hat, went to the hardware store and bought a keg of nails. He took off his hat and the egg dropped into the keg of nails.

The hardware man picked up the egg, put it in *his* hat, and went out to speak to a policeman. He took off his hat, speaking to the policeman, and the egg dropped on the sidewalk.

The policeman picked up the egg and put

it in *his* police hat. The postmaster came past; the policeman took off his police hat and the egg dropped down on the sidewalk.

The postmaster said, "I lost that egg, it is my egg," picked it up, put it in his postmaster's hat, and forgot all about having an egg in his hat.

Then the postmaster, a long tall man, came to the door of the postoffice, a short small door. And the postmaster didn't stoop low, didn't bend under, so he bumped his hat and his head on the top of the doorway. And the egg *broke* and ran down over his face and neck.

And long before that happened, Shush Shush was home in her coop, standing in the door saying, "It is a big day for me because I laid one of my big buff banty eggs in the postmaster's hat."

There Shush Shush stays, living in a coop. Sometimes she marches out of the coop and goes away and lays eggs in pianos, clocks, hats. But she always comes back to the coop.

And whenever she goes to the front door and lays an egg in the door-bell, she rings the bell once for one egg, twice for two eggs, and a dozen rings for a dozen eggs.

3. Five Stories About Hatrack the Horse, Six Pigeons, Three Wild Babylonian Baboons, Six Umbrellas, Bozo the Button Buster.

People: Hatrack the Horse
Peter Potato Blossom Wishes
Rag Bag Mammy
Gimmes

Wiffle the Chick
Chickamauga
Chattanooga
Chattahoochee
Blue Mist
Bubbles
Wednesday Evening in the Twilight and the Gloaming
Telegrams

The Three Wild Babylonian Baboons
Three Umbrellas
The Night Policeman

Six Umbrellas
The Big Umbrella
Straw Hats
Dippy the Wisp

Bozo the Button Buster
A Mouse
Deep Red Roses
The Beans Are Burning
Sweeter Than the Bees Humming

How Rag Bag Mammy Kept Her Secret While the Wind Blew Away the Village of Hat Pins

There was a horse-face man in the Village of Cream Puffs. People called him Hatrack the Horse.

The skin stretched tight over his bones. Once a little girl said, "His eyes look like lightning bugs lighting up the summer night coming out of two little doors."

When Hatrack the Horse took *off* his hat he reached his hand around behind and hung the hat *on* a shoulder bone sticking out.

33

When he wanted to put *on* his hat he reached his hand around and took it *off* from where it was hanging on the shoulder bone sticking out behind.

One summer Hatrack said to Peter Potato Blossom Wishes, "I am going away up north and west in the Rootabaga Country to see the towns different from each other. Then I will come back east as far as I went west, and south as far as I went north, till I am back again where my little pal, Peter Potato Blossom Wishes, lives in the Village of Cream Puffs."

So he went away, going north and west and coming back east and south till he was back again in his home town, sitting on the front steps of his little red shanty, fixing a kite to fly.

"Are you glad to come back?" asked Peter.

"Yes, this is home, this is the only place where I know how the winds act up so I can talk to them when I fly a kite."

"Tell me what you saw and how you listened

34

and if they handed you any nice packages."

"They handed me packages, all right, all right," said Hatrack the Horse.

"Away far to the west I came to the Village of Hat Pins," he went on. "It is the place where they make all the hat pins for the hats to be pinned on in the Rootabaga Country. They asked me about the Village of Cream Puffs and how the winds are here because the winds here blow so many hats off that the Village of Hat Pins sells more hat pins to the people here than anywhere else.

"There is an old woman in the Village of Hat Pins. She walks across the town and around the town every morning and every afternoon. On her back is a big rag bag. She never takes anything out of the rag bag. She never puts anything in. That is, nobody ever sees her put anything in or take anything out. She has never opened the rag bag telling people to take a look and see what is in it. She sleeps

35

with the rag bag for a pillow. So it is always with her and nobody looks into it unless she lets them. And she never lets them.

"Her name? Everybody calls her Rag Bag Mammy. She wears aprons with big pockets. And though she never speaks to big grown-up people she is always glad to meet little growing people, boys and girls. And especially, most of all, she likes to meet boys and girls who say, 'Gimme' (once, like that) or 'Gimme, gimme' (twice, like that) or 'Gimme, gimme, gimme' (three times) or 'Gimme, gimme, gimme, gimme, gimme, gimme' (more times than we can count). She likes to meet the gimmes because she digs into her pockets and brings out square chocolate drops and round chocolate drops and chocolate drops shaped like a half moon, barber pole candy with red and white stripes wrapped around it, all day suckers so long they last not only all day but all this week and all next week, and different kinds of jack-stones, some that say chink-chink on the sidewalks and some that say teentsy-weentsy chink-chink when they all bunch together on the sidewalk. And sometimes if one of the gimmes is crying and feeling bad she gives the gimme a doll only as big as a child's hand but the doll can say the alphabet and sing little Chinese Assyrian songs.

"Of course," said Hatrack the Horse, reaching his hand around to see if his hat was hanging on behind, "of course, you have to have sharp ears and listen close-up and be nice when you are listening, if you are going to hear a doll say the alphabet and sing little Chinese Assyrian songs."

"I could hear them," said Peter Potato Blossom Wishes. "I am a nice listener. I could hear those dolls sing the little Chinese Assyrian songs."

"I believe you, little pal of mine," said Hatrack. "I know you have the ears and you know how to put your ears so you hear."

"Of course, every morning and every afternoon when Rag Bag Mammy walks across the town and around the town in the Village of Hat Pins, people ask her what is in the rag bag on her back. And she answers, 'It is a nice day we are having,' or 'I think the rain will stop when it stops raining, don't you?' Then if they ask again and beg and plead, '*What* is in the rag bag? What *is* in the rag bag?' she tells them, 'When the wind blows away the Village of Hat Pins and blows it so far away it never comes back, then—then, then, then— I will tell you what is in the rag bag.' "

"One day the wind came along and blew the Village of Hat Pins loose, and after blowing it loose, carried it high off in the sky. And the people were saying to each other, 'Well, now we are going to hear Rag Bag Mammy tell us what is in the rag bag.'

"And the wind kept blowing, carrying the Village of Hat Pins higher and farther and farther and higher. And when at last it went away so high it came to a white cloud, the hat pins in the village all stuck out and fastened the village to the cloud so the wind couldn't blow it any farther.

"And—after a while they pulled the hat-pins out of the cloud—and the village dropped back right down where it was before.

"And Rag Bag Mammy goes every morning and every afternoon with the rag bag on her back across and around the town. And sometimes people say to her, 'The next time the wind blows us away—the next time the wind will blow us so far there won't be any cloud to fasten hat pins in—and you will have to tell us what is in the rag bag.' And Rag Bag Mammy just answers, 'Yes, yes—yes—yes,' and goes on her way looking for the next boy or girl to say, 'Gimme' (once, like that) or 'Gimme, gimme' (twice, like that) or 'Gimme, gimme, gimme, gimme, gimme' (more times than we can count).

"And if a child is crying she digs into her pockets and pulls out the doll that says the alphabet and sings little Chinese Assyrian songs."

"And," said Peter Potato Blossom Wishes, "you have to listen close up with your ears and be nice when you are listening."

"In the Village of Hat Pins that the wind nearly blew away forever," said Hatrack the Horse.

And Peter Potato Blossom Wishes skipped away down from the little red shanty, skipped down the street, and then began walking slow saying to herself, "I love Hatrack the Horse like a grand uncle—his eyes look like lightning bugs lighting up the summer night coming out of two little doors."

How Six Pigeons Came Back to Hatrack the Horse After Many Accidents and Six Telegrams

Six crooked ladders stood against the front of the shanty where Hatrack the Horse lived.

Yellow roses all on fire were climbing up and down the ladders, up and down and cross-ways.

And leaning out on both sides from the crooked ladders were vines of yellow roses, leaning, curving, nearly falling.

Hatrack the Horse was waiting. This was the morning Wiffle the Chick was coming.

"Sit here on the cracker box and listen," he said to her when she came; "listen and you will hear the roses saying, 'This is climbing time for all yellow roses and climbing time is the time to climb; how did we ever learn to climb only by climbing? Listen and you will hear—st..th..st..th..st..th..it is the feet of the yellow roses climbing up and down and leaning out and curving and nearly falling ..st..th..st..th..' "

So Wiffle the Chick sat there, early in the summer, enjoying herself, sitting on a cracker box, listening to the yellow roses climb around the six crooked ladders.

Hatrack the Horse came out. On his shoulders were two pigeons, on his hands two pigeons. And he reached his hand around behind his back where his hat was hanging and he opened the hat and showed Wiffle the Chick two pigeons in the hat.

"They are lovely pigeons to look at and their

42

eyes are full of lessons to learn," said Wiffle the Chick. "Maybe you will tell me why you have their feet wrapped in bandages, hospital liniment bandages full of hospital liniment smells? Why do you put soft mittens on the feet of these pigeons so lovely to look at?"

"They came back yesterday, they came back home," was the answer. "They came back limping on their feet with the toes turned in so far they nearly turned backward. When they put their bleeding feet in my hands one by one each one, it was like each one was writing his name in my hand with red ink."

"Did you know they were coming?" asked Wiffle.

"Every day the last six days I get a telegram, six telegrams from six pigeons—and at last they come home. And ever since they come home they are telling me they come because they love Hatrack the Horse and the yellow climbing roses climbing over the six crooked ladders."

"Did you name your pigeons with names?" asked Wiffle.

"These three, the sandy and golden brown, all named themselves by where they came from. This is Chickamauga, here is Chattanooga, and this is Chattahoochee. And the other three all got their names from me when I was feeling high and easy. This is Blue Mist, here is Bubbles, and last of all take a look at Wednesday Evening in the Twilight and the Gloaming."

"Do you always call her Wednesday Evening in the Twilight and the Gloaming?"

"Not when I am making coffee for breakfast. If I am making coffee for breakfast then I just call her Wednesday Evening."

"Didn't you tie the mittens on her feet extra special nice?"

"Yes—she is an extra special nice pigeon. She cries for pity when she wants pity. And she shuts her eyes when she doesn't want to look at you. And if you look deep in her eyes

44

when her eyes are open you will see lights there exactly like the lights on the pastures and the meadows when the mist is drifting on a Wednesday evening just between the twilight and the gloaming.

"A week ago yesterday they all went away. And they won't tell why they went away. Somebody clipped their wings, cut off their flying feathers so they couldn't fly—and they won't tell why. They were six hundred miles from home—but they won't tell how they counted the six hundred miles. A hundred miles a day they walked, six hundred miles in a week, and they sent a telegram to me every day, one writing a telegram one day and another writing a telegram the next day—all the time walking a hundred miles a day with their toes turned in like pigeon toes turn in. Do you wonder they needed bandages, hospital liniment bandages on their feet—and soft mittens?"

"Show me the telegrams they sent you, one

every day, for six days while they were walking six hundred miles on their pigeon toes."

So Hatrack the Horse got the six telegrams. The reading on the telegrams was like this:

1. "Feet are as good as wings if you have to. CHICKAMAUGA."

2. "If you love to go somewhere it is easy to walk. CHATTANOOGA."

3. "In the night sleeping you forget whether you have wings or feet or neither. CHATTAHOOCHEE."

4. "What are toes for if they don't point to what you want? BLUE MIST."

5. "Anybody can walk hundreds of miles putting one foot ahead of the other. BUBBLES."

6. "Pity me. Far is far. Near is near. And there is no place like home when the yellow roses climb up the ladders and sing in the early summer. Pity me. WEDNESDAY EVENING IN THE TWILIGHT AND THE GLOAMING."

"Did they have any accidents going six hundred miles walking with their little pigeon toes turned in?" asked Wiffle.

"Once they had an accident," said Hatrack, with Chattahoochee standing in his hat, Chickamauga on his right shoulder, Chattanooga on his left, and holding Blue Mist and Bubbles on his wrists. "They came to an old wooden bridge. Chattahoochee and Wednesday Evening both cried out, 'The bridge will fall if we all walk on it the same time!' But they were all six already on the bridge and the bridge began sagging and tumbled them all into the river. But it was good for them all to have a footbath for their feet, Wednesday Evening explained."

"I got a suspicion you like Wednesday Evening in the Twilight and the Gloaming best of all," spoke up Wiffle.

"Well, Wednesday Evening was the only one I noticed making any mention of the yellow roses in her telegram," Hatrack the

47

Horse explained, as he picked up Wednesday Evening and reached her around and put her to perch on the shoulder bone on his back.

Then the old man and the girl sat on the cracker box saying nothing, only listening to the yellow roses all on fire with early summer climbing up the crooked ladders, up and down and crossways, some of them leaning out and curving and nearly falling.

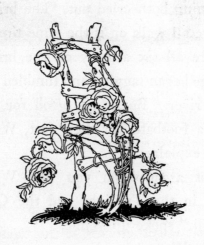

How the Three Wild Babylonian Baboons Went Away in the Rain Eating Bread and Butter

One morning when Hatrack the Horse went away from his shanty, he put three umbrellas in the corner next to the front door.

His pointing finger pointed at the three umbrellas as he said, "If the three wild Babylonian Baboons come sneaking up to this shanty and sneaking through the door and sneaking through the house, then all you three umbrellas open up like it was raining, jump straight at the baboons and fasten your handles in their hands. Then, all three of you stay open as if it was raining—and hold those handles in the hands of the baboons and never let go till I come."

Hatrack the Horse went away. The three umbrellas stood in the corner next to the front door. And when the umbrellas listened they could hear the three wild Babylonian Baboons sneaking up to the shanty. Soon the baboons, all hairy all over, bangs down their foreheads, came sneaking through the door. Just as they were sneaking through the door they took off their hats to show they were getting ready to sneak through the house.

Then the three umbrellas in the corner opened up as if it was raining; they jumped straight at the three wild Babylonian Baboons;

50

and they fastened their handles tight in the hands of the baboons and wouldn't let go.

So there were the three wild Babylonian Baboons, each with a hat in his left hand, and an open umbrella in his right hand.

When Hatrack the Horse came home he came, quiet. He opened the front door, quiet. Then he looked around inside the house, quiet.

In the corner where he had stood the three umbrellas, he saw the three wild Babylonian Baboons on the floor, sleeping, with umbrellas over their faces.

"The umbrellas were so big they couldn't get through the door," said Hatrack the Horse. For a long time he stood looking at the bangs hanging down the foreheads of the baboons while they were sleeping. He took a comb and combed the bangs down the foreheads of the baboons. He went to the cupboard and spread bread and butter. He took the hats out of the left hands of the baboons

51

and put the hats on their heads. He put a piece of bread and butter in the hand of each baboon.

After that he snipped each one across the nose with his finger (*snippety-snip!* just like that). They opened their eyes and stood up. Then he loosened the umbrella handles from their right hands and led them to the door.

They all looked out. It was raining. "Now you can go," he told the baboons. And they all walked out of the front door, and they seemed to be snickering and hiding the snickers.

The last he saw of them they were walking away in the rain eating bread and butter. And they took off their hats so the rain ran down and slid off on the bangs of their fore-heads.

Hatrack the Horse turned to the umbrellas and said, "We know how to make a surprise party when we get a visit from the Babylonian

Baboons with their bangs falling down their foreheads—don't we?"

That is what happened, as Hatrack the Horse told it to the night policeman in the Village of Cream Puffs.

How Six Umbrellas Took Off Their Straw Hats to Show Respect to the One Big Umbrella

Wherever Dippy the Wisp went she was always changing hats. She carried two hat boxes with big picture hats on her *right* arm. And she carried two hat boxes with big picture hats on her *left* arm. And she changed from green and gold hats to purple and gray hats and then back to green and gold whenever she felt like it.

Now the hill that runs down from the shanty of Hatrack the Horse toward the Village of Cream Puffs is a long, long hill. And one morning the old man sat watching and away down at the bottom of the long, long hill he saw four hat boxes. Somebody was coming to call on him. And he knew it was Dippy the Wisp.

The hat boxes came up the hill. He saw them stop once, stop twice, stop more times. So he knew Dippy the Wisp was changing hats, changing from green and gold to purple and gray and then back to green and gold.

When at last she got to the top of the hill and came to the shanty of Hatrack the Horse, she said to him, "Make up a story and tell me. Make up the story about umbrellas. You have traveled all over the Rootabaga Country, you have seen so many umbrellas, and such wonderful umbrellas. Make me up a big elegant story about umbrellas."

So Hatrack the Horse took his hat *off* his head, reached around and hung it *on* one of the shoulder bones sticking out behind on his back. And the old man looked with a far-away look down the long, long hill running from his shanty toward the Village of Cream Puffs. Then he told her this story:

One summer afternoon I came home and found all the umbrellas sitting in the kitchen, with straw hats on, telling each other who they are.

The umbrella that feeds the fishes fresh buns every morning stood up and said, "I am the umbrella that feeds the fishes fresh buns every morning."

The umbrella that fixes the clocks free of charge stood up and said, "I am the umbrella that fixes the clocks free of charge."

The umbrella that peels the potatoes with a

57

pencil and makes a pink ink with the peelings, stood up and said, "I am the umbrella that peels the potatoes with a pencil and makes a pink ink with the peelings."

The umbrella that eats the rats with pepper and salt and a clean napkin every morning, stood up and said, "I am the umbrella that eats the rats with pepper and salt and a clean napkin every morning."

The umbrella that washes the dishes with a wiper and wipes the dishes with a washer every morning stood up and said, "I am the umbrella that washes the dishes with a wiper and wipes the dishes with a washer every morning."

The umbrella that covers the chimney with a dishpan before it rains stood up and said, "I am the umbrella that covers the chimney with a dishpan before it rains."

The umbrella that runs to the corner to get corners for the handkerchiefs stood up and said, "I am the umbrella that runs to the corner to get corners for the handkerchiefs."

Now while the umbrellas are all sitting in the kitchen with their straw hats on telling each other who they are, there comes a big black stranger of an umbrella, walking into the kitchen without opening the door, walking in without knocking, without asking anybody, without telling anybody beforehand.

"Since we are telling each other who we are," said the stranger, "since we are telling each other who we are, I am going to tell you who I am.

"I am the umbrella that holds up the sky. I am the umbrella the rain comes through. I am the umbrella that tells the sky when to begin raining and when to stop raining.

"I am the umbrella that goes to pieces when the wind blows and then puts itself together again when the wind goes down. I am the first umbrella, the last umbrella, the one and only umbrella all other umbrellas are named after, first, last and always."

When the stranger finished this speech telling who he was and where he came from, all the other umbrellas sat still for a little while, to be respectful.

Then they all got up, took off their straw hats, walked up to the stranger and laid those straw hats at his feet. They wanted to show him they had respect for him. Then they all walked out, first the umbrella that feeds the fishes fresh buns every morning, then the umbrella that fixes the clocks free of charge, then the umbrella that peels the potatoes with a pencil and makes pink ink with the peelings, then the umbrella that eats the rats with pepper and salt and a clean napkin, then the umbrella that washes the dishes with a wiper and wipes the dishes with a washer, then the umbrella that covers the chimney with a dish-pan before it rains, then the umbrella that

60

runs to the corner to get corners for the handkerchiefs. They all laid their straw hats at
the feet of the stranger because he came without knocking or telling anybody beforehand
and because he said he is the umbrella that
holds up the sky, that big umbrella the rain
goes through first of all, the first and the last
umbrella.

That was the way Hatrack the Horse finished his story for Dippy the Wisp. She was
changing hats, getting ready to go.

The old man put his loose bony arms around
her and kissed her for a good-by. And she
put her little dimpled arms around his neck
and kissed him for a good-by.

And the last he saw of her that day she was
walking far away down at the bottom of the
long, long hill that stretches from Hatrack's
shanty toward the Village of Cream Puffs.

And twice going down the long hill she

stopped and changed hats, opening and shutting the hat boxes, and changing hats from green and gold to purple and gray and back to green and gold.

How Bozo the Button Buster Busted All His Buttons When a Mouse Came

One summer evening the stars in the summer sky seemed to be moving with fishes, cats and rabbits.

It was that summer evening three girls came to the shanty of Hatrack the Horse. He asked each one, "What is your name?" And they answered; first, "Me? My name is Deep Red Roses"; second, "Me? My name is The Beans are Burning"; and last of all, "Me? My name is Sweeter Than the Bees Humming."

And the old man fastened a yellow rose for luck in the hair of each one and said, "You ought to be home now."

"After you tell us a story," they reminded him.

"I can only tell you a sad story all mixed up to-night," he reminded them, "because all day to-day I have been thinking about Bozo the Button Buster."

"Tell us about Bozo the Button Buster," said the girls, feeling in their hair and fixing the yellow roses.

The old man sat down on the front steps. His eyes swept away off toward a corner of the sky heavy with mist where it seemed to be moving with firetails, fishes, cats, and rabbits of slow changing stars.

"Bozo had buttons all over him," said the old man, "the buttons on Bozo fitted so tight, and there were so many buttons, that sometimes when he took his lungs full of new wind to go

64

on talking a button would bust loose and fly into the face of whoever he was speaking to. Sometimes when he took new wind into his lungs two buttons would bust loose and fly into the faces of two people he was speaking to.

"So people said, 'Isn't it queer how buttons fly loose when Bozo fills his lungs with wind to go on speaking?' After a while everybody called him Bozo the Button Buster.

"Now, you must understand, Bozo was different from other people. He had a string tied to him. It was a long string hanging down with a knot in the end. He used to say, 'Sometimes I forget where I am; then I feel for the string tied to me, and I follow the string to where it is tied to me; then I know where I am again.'

"Sometimes when Bozo was speaking and a button busted loose, he would ask, 'Was that a mouse? Was that a mouse?' And sometimes he said to people, 'I'll talk with you— *if you haven't got a mouse in your pocket.*'

65

How Bozo the Button Buster Busted

"The last day Bozo ever came to the Village of Cream Puffs, he stood on the public square and he was all covered with buttons, more buttons than ever before, and all the buttons fitting tight, and five, six buttons busting loose and flying into the air whenever he took his lungs full of wind to go on speaking.

" 'When the sky began to fall who was it ran out and held up the sky?' he sang out. 'It was me, it was me ran out and held up the sky when the sky began to fall.'

" 'When the blue came off the sky, where did they get the blue to put on the sky to make it blue again? It was me, it was me picked the bluebirds and the blue pigeons to get the blue to fix the sky.'

" 'When it rains now it rains umbrellas first so everybody has an umbrella for the rain afterward. Who fixed that? I did—Bozo the Button Buster.'

" 'Who took the rainbow off the sky and put it back again in a hurry? That was me.'

The mouse bit the knot and cut it loose

" 'Who turned all the barns upside down and then put them right side up again? I did that.'

" 'Who took the salt out of the sea and put it back again? Who took the fishes out of the sea and put them back again? That was me.'

" 'Who started the catfish fighting the cats? Who made the slippery elms slippery? Who made the King of the Broken Bottles a wanderer wandering over the world mumbling, "Easy, easy"? Who opened the windows of the stars and threw fishes, cats and rabbits all over the frames of the sky? I did, I did, I did.'

"All the time Bozo kept on speaking the buttons kept on busting because he had to stop so often to fill his lungs with new wind to go on speaking. The public square was filled with piles of buttons that kept busting off from Bozo the Button Buster that day.

"And at last a mouse came, a sneaking, slippery, quick little mouse. He ran with a flash

to the string tied to Bozo, the long string hanging down with a knot in the end. He bit the
knot and cut it loose. He slit the string with
his teeth as Bozo cried, 'Ai! Ai! Ai!'

"The last of all the buttons busted loose off
Bozo. The clothes fell off. The people came
up to see what was happening to Bozo. There
was nothing in the clothes. The man inside
the clothes was gone. All that was left was
buttons and a few clothes.

"Since then whenever it rains umbrellas
first so everybody has an umbrella for the rain
afterward, or if the sky looks like it is falling,
or if a barn turns upside down, or if the King
of the Broken Bottles comes along mumbling,
'Easy, easy,' or if firetails, fishes, cats and rabbits come on the sky in the night, or if a button
busts loose and flies into somebody's face, people remember Bozo the Button Buster."

When the three girls started home, each one

said to Hatrack the Horse, "It looks dark and lonesome on the prairie, but you put a yellow rose in my hair for luck—and I won't be scared after I get home."

4. Two Stories About Four Boys Who Had Different Dreams.

People: Googler
Gaggler
Twins
The Family Doctor
The Father of the Twins
The Mother of the Twins
Pen Wipers and Pencil Sharpeners
Smokestacks and Monkey Wrenches
Monkey Faces on the Monkey Wrenches
Left-Handed Monkey Wrenches

Potato Face Blind Man
Ax Me No Questions
Johnny the Wham
Joe the Wimp
Grasshoppers
Thousand Dollar Bills
Brass Doors
Lizzie Lazarus

How Googler and Gaggler, the Two Christmas Babies, Came Home with Monkey Wrenches

1

Two babies came one night in snowstorm weather, came to a tar paper shack on a cinder patch next the railroad yards on the edge of the Village of Liver-and-Onions.

The family doctor came that night, came with a bird of a spizz car throwing a big spotlight of a headlight through the snow of the snowstorm on the prairie.

"Twins," said the doctor. "Twins," said

the father and mother. And the wind as it shook the tar paper shack and shook the doors and the padlocks on the doors of the tar paper shack, the wind seemed to be howling softly, "Twins, twins."

Six days and Christmas Eve came. The mother of the twins lit two candles, two little two-for-a-nickel candles in each little window. And the mother handed the father the twins and said, "Here are your Christmas presents." The father took the two baby boys and laughed, "Twice times twice is twice."

The two little two-for-a-nickel candles sputtered in each little window that Christmas Eve, and at last sputtered and went out, leaving the prairies dark and lonesome. The father and the mother of the twins sat by the window, each one holding a baby.

Every once in a while they changed babies so as to hold a different twin. And every time they changed they laughed at each other, "Twice times twice is twice."

One baby was called Googler, the other Gaggler. The two boys grew up, and hair came on their bald red heads. Their ears, wet behind, got dry. They learned how to pull on their stockings and shoes and tie their shoe-strings. They learned at last how to take a handkerchief and hold it open and blow their noses.

Their father looked at them growing up and said, "I think you'll make a couple of peanut-wagon men pouring hot butter into popcorn sacks."

The family doctor saw the rashes and the itches and the measles and the whooping cough come along one year and another. He saw the husky Googler and the husky Gaggler throw off the rashes and the itches and the measles and the whooping cough. And the family doctor said, "They will go far and see much, and they will never be any good for sitting with the sitters and knitting with the knitters."

Googler and Gaggler grew up and turned

handsprings going to school in short pants, whistling with school books under their arms. They went barefooted and got stickers in their hair and teased cats and killed snakes and climbed apple trees and threw clubs up walnut trees and chewed slippery ellum. They stubbed their toes and cut their feet on broken bottles and went swimming in brickyard ponds and came home with their backs sunburnt so the skin peeled off. And before they went to bed every night they stood on their heads and turned flip-flops.

One morning early in spring the young frogs were shooting silver spears of little new songs up into the sky. Strips of fresh young grass were beginning to flick the hills and spot the prairie with flicks and spots of new green. On that morning, Googler and Gaggler went to school with fun and danger and dreams in their eyes.

They came home that day and told their mother, "There is a war between the pen wipers and the pencil sharpeners. Millions of pen wipers and millions of pencil sharpeners are marching against each other, marching and singing, *Hayfoot, strawfoot, bellyful o' bean soup.* The pen wipers and the pencil sharpeners, millions and millions, are marching with drums, drumming, *Ta rum, ta rum, ta rum tum tum.* The pen wipers say, No matter how many million ink spots it costs and no matter how many million pencil sharpeners we kill, we are going to kill and kill till the last of the pencil sharpeners is killed. The pencil sharpeners say, No matter how many million shavings it costs, no matter how many million pen wipers we kill, we are going to kill and kill till the last of the pen wipers is killed."

The mother of Googler and Gaggler listened, her hands folded, her thumbs under her chin, her eyes watching the fun and the danger and the dreams in the eyes of the two boys. And she said, "Me, oh, my—but those pen

wipers and pencil sharpeners hate each other."
And she turned her eyes toward the flicks and
spots of new green grass coming on the hills
and the prairie, and she let her ears listen to
the young frogs shooting silver spears of little
songs up into the sky that day.

And she told her two boys, "Pick up your
feet now and run. Go to the grass, go to the
new green grass. Go to the young frogs and
ask them why they are shooting songs up into
the sky this early spring day. Pick up your
feet now and run."

2

At last Googler and Gaggler were big boys,
big enough to pick the stickers out of each
other's hair, big enough to pick up their feet
and run away from anybody who chased them.

One night they turned flip-flops and handsprings and climbed up on top of a peanut
wagon where a man was pouring hot butter

They went to sleep on top of the wagon

into popcorn sacks. They went to sleep on top of the wagon. Googler dreamed of teasing cats, killing snakes, climbing apple trees and stealing apples. Gaggler dreamed of swimming in brickyard ponds and coming home with his back sunburnt so the skin peeled off.

They woke up with heavy gunnysacks in their arms. They climbed off the wagon and started home to their father and mother lugging the heavy gunnysacks on their backs. And they told their father and mother:

"We ran away to the Thimble Country where the people wear thimble hats, where the women wash dishes in thimble dishpans, where the men go to work with thimble shovels.

"We saw a war, the left-handed people against the right-handed. And the smokestacks did all the fighting. They all had monkey wrenches and they tried to wrench each other to pieces. And they had monkey faces on the monkey wrenches—to scare each other.

"All the time they were fighting the Thimble people sat looking on, the thimble women with thimble dishpans, the thimble men with thimble shovels. They waved handkerchiefs to each other, some left-hand handkerchiefs, and some right-hand handkerchiefs. They sat looking till the smokestacks with their monkey wrenches wrenched each other all to pieces."

Then Googler and Gaggler opened the heavy gunnysacks. "Here," they said, "here is a left-handed monkey wrench, here is a right-handed monkey wrench. And here is a monkey wrench with a monkey face on the handle—to scare with."

Now the father and mother of Googler and Gaggler wonder how they will end up. The family doctor keeps on saying, "They will go far and see much but they will never sit with the sitters and knit with the knitters." And sometimes when their father looks at them, he says what he said the Christmas Eve when the two-for-a-nickel candles stood two by two in the windows, "Twice times twice is twice."

How Johnny the Wham Sleeps in Money All the Time and Joe the Wimp Shines and Sees Things

Once the Potato Face Blind Man began talking about arithmetic and geography, where numbers come from and why we add and subtract before we multiply, when the first fractions and decimal points were invented, who gave the rivers their names, and why some rivers have short names slipping off the tongue easy as whistling, and why other rivers have long names wearing the stub ends off lead pencils.

How Johnny the Wham

The girl, Ax Me No Questions, asked the old man if boys always stay in the home towns where they are born and grow up, or whether boys pack their packsacks and go away somewhere else after they grow up. This question started the old man telling about Johnny the Wham and Joe the Wimp and things he remembered about them:

Johnny the Wham and Joe the Wimp are two boys who used to live here in the Village of Liver-and-Onions before they went away. They grew up here, carving their initials, J. W., on wishbones and peanuts and wheelbarrows. And if anybody found a wishbone or a peanut or a wheelbarrow with the initials, J. W., carved on it, he didn't know whether it was Johnny the Wham or Joe the Wimp.

They met on summer days, put their hands in their pockets and traded each other grasshoppers learning to say yes and no. One kick and a spit meant yes. Two kicks and a spit meant no. One two three, four five six of a kick and a spit meant the grasshopper was counting and learning numbers.

They promised what they were going to do after they went away from the village. Johnny the Wham said, "I am going to sleep in money up to my knees with thousand dollar bills all over me for a blanket." Joe the Wimp said, "I am going to see things and shine, and I am going to shine and see things."

They went away. They did what they said. They went up into the grasshopper country near the Village of Eggs Over where the grasshoppers were eating the corn in the fields without counting how much. They stayed in those fields till those grasshoppers learned to say yes and no and learned to count. One kick and a spit meant yes. Two kicks and a spit meant no. One two three, four five six meant the grasshoppers were counting and learning numbers. The grasshoppers, after that, eating ears of corn in the fields, were counting how many and how much.

To-day Johnny the Wham sleeps in a room full of money in the big bank in the Village of Eggs Over. The room where he sleeps is the room where they keep the thousand dollar bills. He walks in thousand dollar bills up to his knees at night before he goes to bed on the floor. A bundle of thousand dollar bills is his pillow. He covers himself like a man in a haystack or a strawstack, with thousand dollar bills. The paper money is piled around him in armfuls and sticks up and stands out around him the same as hay or straw.

And Lizzie Lazarus, who talked with him in the Village of Eggs Over last week, she says Johnny the Wham told her, "There is music in thousand dollar bills. Before I go to sleep at night and when I wake up in the morning, I listen to their music. They whisper and cry, they sing little oh-me, oh-my songs as they wriggle and rustle next to each other. A few with dirty faces, with torn ears, with patches and finger and thumb prints on their faces, they cry and whisper so it hurts to hear them. And often they shake all over, laughing.

"I heard one dirty thousand dollar bill say to another spotted with patches and thumb prints, 'They kiss us welcome when we come, they kiss us sweet good-by when we go.'

"They cry and whisper and laugh about things and special things and extra extra special things—pigeons, ponies, pigs, special pigeons, ponies, pigs, extra extra special pigeons, ponies, pigs—cats, pups, monkeys, big bags of cats, pups, monkeys, extra extra big bags of special cats, pups, monkeys—jewelry, ice cream, bananas, pie, hats, shoes, shirts, dust pans, rat traps, coffee cups, handkerchiefs, safety pins—diamonds, bottles and big front doors with bells on—they cry and whisper and laugh about these things—and it never hurts unless the dirty thousand dollar bills with torn ears and patches on their faces say to each other,

91

'They kiss us welcome when we come, they kiss us sweet good-by when we go.' "

The old Potato Face sat saying nothing. He fooled a little with the accordion keys as if trying to make up a tune for the words, "They kiss us welcome when we come, they kiss us sweet good-by when we go."

Ax Me No Questions looked at him with a soft look and said softly, "Now maybe you'll tell about Joe the Wimp." And he told her:

Joe the Wimp shines the doors in front of the bank. The doors are brass, and Joe the Wimp stands with rags and ashes and chamois skin keeping the brass shining.

"The brass shines slick and shows everything on the street like a looking glass," he told Lizzie Lazarus last week. "If pigeons, ponies, pigs, come past, or cats, pups, monkeys, or jewelry, ice cream, bananas, pie, hats, shoes, shirts, dust pans, rat traps, coffee cups, handkerchiefs, safety pins, or diamonds, bottles, and big front doors with bells on, Joe the Wimp sees them in the brass.

"I rub on the brass doors, and things begin to jump into my hands out of the shine of the brass. Faces, chimneys, elephants, yellow humming birds, and blue cornflowers, where I have seen grasshoppers sleeping two by two and two by two, they all come to the shine of the brass on the doors when I ask them to. If you shine brass hard, and wish as hard as the brass wishes, and keep on shining and wishing, then always things come jumping into your hands out of the shine of the brass."

"So you see," said the Potato Face Blind Man to Ax Me No Questions, "sometimes the promises boys make when they go away come true afterward."

"They got what they asked for—now will they keep it or leave it?" said Ax Me.

"Only the grasshoppers can answer that,"

was the old man's reply. "The grasshoppers are older. They know more about jumps. And especially grasshoppers that say yes and no and count one two three, four five six."

And he sat saying nothing, fooling with the accordion keys as if trying to make up a tune for the words, "They kiss us welcome when we come, they kiss us sweet good-by when we go."

5. Two Stories Told by the Potato
   Face Blind Man About Two Girls
   with Red Hearts.

People: Blixie Bimber
The Potato Face Blind Man
Shoulder Straps
High High Over
Six Bits
Deep Red Roses
A Clock
A Looking Glass
Baggage

Pink Peony
Spuds the Ballplayer
Four Moon
Peacocks
Frogs
Oranges
Yellow Silk Handkerchiefs

How Deep Red Roses Goes Back and Forth Between the Clock and the Looking Glass

One morning when big white clouds were shouldering each other's shoulders, rolling on the rollers of a big blue sky, Blixie Bimber came along where the Potato Face Blind Man sat shining the brass bickerjiggers on his accordion.

"Do you like to shine up the brass bickerjiggers?" asked Blixie.

97

"Yes," he answered. "One time a long time ago the brass bickerjiggers were gold, but they stole the gold away when I wasn't looking."

He blinked the eyelids over his eyeballs and said, "I thank them because they took gold they wanted. Brass feels good to my fingers the same as gold." And he went on shining up the brass bickerjiggers on the accordion, humming a little line of an old song, "To-morrow will never catch up with yesterday because yesterday started sooner."

"Seems like a nice morning with the sun spilling bushels of sunshine," he said to Blixie, who answered, "Big white clouds are shouldering each other's shoulders rolling on the rollers of a big blue sky."

"Seems like it's April all over again," he murmured, almost like he wasn't talking at all.

"Seems just that way—April all over again," murmured Blixie, almost like she wasn't talking at all.

So they began drifting, the old man drifting his way, the girl drifting her way, till he drifted into a story. And the story he told was like this and in these words:

"Deep Red Roses was a lovely girl with blue skylights like the blue skylights of early April in her eyes. And her lips reminded people of deep red roses waiting in the cool of the summer evening.

"She met Shoulder Straps one day when she was young yet. He promised her. And she promised him. But he went away. One of the long wars between two short wars took him. In a far away country, then, he married another girl. And he didn't come back to Deep Red Roses.

"Next came High High Over, one day when she was young yet. A dancer he was, going from one city to another city to dance, spending his afternoons and evenings and late nights dancing, and sleeping in the morning till noon. And when he promised she promised. But he went away to another city and after that another city. And he married one woman and then another woman. Every year there came a new story about one of the new wives of High High Over, the dancer. And while she was young yet, Deep Red Roses forgot all about her promise and the promise of High High Over, the dancer who ran away from her.

"Six Bits was the next to come along. And he was not a soldier nor a dancer nor anything special. He was a careless man, changing from one job to another, changing from paperhanging to plastering, from fixing shingle roofs where the shingles were ripped to opening cans with can openers.

"Six Bits gave Deep Red Roses his promise and she gave him her promise. But he was always late keeping his promise. When the wedding was to be Tuesday he didn't come till Wednesday. If it was Friday he came Saturday. And there wasn't any wedding.

"So Deep Red Roses said to herself, 'I am going away and learn, I am going away and talk with the wives of High High Over, the dancer, and maybe if I go far enough I will find the wife of Shoulder Straps, the soldier—and maybe the wives of the men who promised me will tell me how to keep promises kept.'

"She packed her baggage till her baggage was packed so full there was room for only one more thing. So she had to decide whether to put a *clock* or whether to put a *looking glass* in her baggage.

" 'My head tells me to carry the clock so I can always tell if I am early or late,' she said to herself. 'But my heart tells me to carry a looking glass so I can look at my face and tell if I am getting older or younger.'

"At last she decides to take the clock and

leave the looking glass—because her head says so. She starts away. She goes through the door, she is out of the house, she goes to the street, she starts up the street.

"Then her heart tells her to go back and change the clock for the looking glass. She goes back up the street, through the door, into the house, into her room. Now she stands in front of the clock and the looking glass saying, 'To-night I sleep home here one more night, and to-morrow morning I decide again.'

"And now every morning Deep Red Roses decides with her head to take the clock. She takes the clock and starts away and then comes back because her heart decides she must have the looking glass.

"If you go to her house this morning you will see her standing in the doorway with blue skylights like the blue sky of early April in her eyes, and lips that remind you of deep red roses in the cool of the evening in summer.

You will see her leave the doorway and go out of the gate with the clock in her hands. Then if you wait you will see her come back through the gate, into the door, back to her room where she puts down the clock and takes up the looking glass.

"After that she decides to wait until to-morrow morning to decide again what to decide. Her head tells her one thing, her heart tells her another. Between the two she stays home. Sometimes she looks at her face in the looking glass and says to herself, 'I am young yet and while I am young I am going to do my own deciding.'"

Blixie Bimber fingered the end of her chin with her little finger and said, "It is a strange story. It has a stab in it. It would hurt me if I couldn't look up at the big white clouds shouldering their shoulders, rolling on the rollers of the big blue sky."

Deep Red Roses Goes Back and Forth

"It is a good story to tell when April is here all over again—and I am shining up the brass bickerjiggers on my accordion," said the Potato Face Blind Man.

How Pink Peony Sent Spuds, the Ball-player, Up to Pick Four Moons

Early one summer evening the moon was hanging in the tree-tops. There was a lisp of leaves. And the soft shine of the moon sifting down seemed to have something to say to the lisp of the leaves.

The girl named Blixie Bimber came that particular summer evening to the corner where the Potato Face Blind Man sat with his accordion. She came walking slow and thoughtful to where he was sitting in the evening shadows. And she told him about the summer moon in the tree-tops, the lisp of the leaves, and the shine of the moon trying to tell something to the lisp of the leaves.

The old man leaned back, fumbled the keys of his accordion, and said it loosened up things he remembered far back.

"On an evening like this, every tree has a moon all of its own for itself—if you climb up in a thousand trees this evening you can pick a thousand moons," the old man murmured. "You remind me to-night about secrets swimming deep in me."

And after hesitating a little—and thinking a little—and then hesitating some more—the old man started and told this story:

There was a girl I used to know, one time, named Pink Peony. She was a girl with cheeks and lips the peonies talked about.

When she passed a bush of peonies, some of

the flowers would whisper, "She is lovelier than we are." And the other peonies would answer in a whisper, "It *must* be so, it . . must . . be . . *so*."

Now there was a ballplayer named Spuds, came one night to take her riding, out to a valley where the peacocks always cry before it rains, where the frogs always gamble with the golden dice after midnight.

And out in that valley they came to a tall tree shooting spraggly to the sky. And high up in the spraggly shoots, where the lisp of the leaves whispers, there a moon had drifted down and was caught in the branches.

"Spuds, climb up and pick *that* moon for me," Pink Peony sang reckless. And the ballplayer jumped out of the car, climbed up the tall tree, up and up till he was high and far in the spraggly branches where the moon had drifted down and was caught.

Climbing down, he handed the girl a silver

hat full of peach-color pearls. She laid it on the back seat of the car where it would be safe. And they drove on.

They came to another tall tree shooting spraggly to the sky. And high up the moon was caught.

"Pick *that* one, Spuds," Peony sang reckless again. And when he came climbing down he handed her a circle of gold with a blood-color autumn leaf. And they put it on the back seat of the car where it would be safe. Then they drove on.

"Spuds, you are good to me," said Pink Peony, when he climbed another tree shooting spraggly high in the sky, and came down with a brass pansy sprinkled with two rainbows, for her. She put it on the back seat where it would be safe. And they drove on.

One time more Spuds climbed up and came down with what he picked, up where the moon was caught in the high spraggly branches. "An Egyptian collar frozen in diamond cobwebs, for you," he said. "You are a dear, Spuds," she said, reckless, with a look into his eyes. She laid the Egyptian collar frozen in diamond cobwebs on the back seat of the car where it would be safe—and they drove on.

They listened a while, they stopped the car and listened a longer while, to the frogs gambling with golden dice after midnight.

And when at last they heard the peacocks crying, they knew it was going to rain. So they drove home.

And while the peacocks were crying, and just before they started home, they looked in the back seat of the car at the silver hat full of peach-color pearls, the circle of gold with a blood-color autumn leaf, the brass pansy sprinkled with two rainbows, the Egyptian collar frozen in diamond cobwebs.

Driving home, the spray of a violet dawn was on the east sky. And it was nearly daylight when they drove up to the front door of

Pink Peony's home. She ran into the house to get a basket to carry the presents in. She came running out of the house with a basket to carry the presents in.

She looked in the back seat; she felt with her hands and fingers all over the back seat.

In the back seat she could find only four oranges. They opened the oranges and in each orange they found a yellow silk handkerchief.

To-day, if you go to the house where Pink Peony and Spuds are living, you will find four children playing there, each with a yellow silk handkerchief tied around the neck in a mystic slip knot.

Each child has a moon face and a moon name. And sometimes their father and mother pile them all into a car and they ride out to the valley where the peacocks always cry before it rains—and where the frogs always gamble with golden dice after midnight.

And what they look longest at is a summer moon hanging in the tree-tops, when there is a lisp of leaves, and the shine of the moon and the lisp of the leaves seem to be telling each other something.

So the Potato Face came to a finish with his story. Blixie Bimber kissed him good-night on the nose, saying, "You loosened up beautiful to-night."

6. Three Stories About Moonlight, Pigeons, Bees, Egypt, Jesse James, Spanish Onions, the Queen of the Cracked Heads, the King of the Paper Sacks.

People: Dippy the Wisp
Slip Me Liz
The Potato Face Blind Man
Egypt
Jesse James
Spanish Onions
The Queen of the Cracked Heads
The King of the Paper Sacks
The Queen of the Empty Hats
Hot Balloons
A Snoox
A Gringo
Sweetheart Dippies
Nail-eating Rats
Sooners
Boomers

More People:
Cracked Heads
Clock-eating Goats
Baby Alligators
Pink and Purple Peanuts
Empty Hats
Bats, Cats, Rats
Rag Pickers, Rag Handlers
Squirrels, Fish, Baboons, Black Cats
A Steel Car, an Air Car
Gophers

How Dippy the Wisp and Slip Me Liz Came in the Moonshine Where the Potato Face Blind Man Sat with His Accordion

The sky shook a rain down one Saturday night over the people, the postoffice, and the peanut-stand in the Village of Liver-and-Onions.

And after the rain, the sky shook loose a moon so a moonshine came with gold on the rain-pools.

And a west wind came out of the west sky and shook the moonshine gold on the tops of the rainpools.

Dippy the Wisp and Slip Me Liz came, two tough pony girls, two limber prairie girls, in the moonshine humming little humpty dumpty songs.

They came to the postoffice corner where the Potato Face Blind Man sat hugging his accordion, wondering what was next and who and why.

He was saying to himself, "Who was it told me the rats on the moon in the middle of the winter lock their mittens in ice boxes?"

And just then Dippy the Wisp and Slip Me Liz came flipping along saying, "It is a misty moisty evening in the moonshine, isn't it?"

And he answered, "The moon is a round gold door with silver transoms to-night. Bumble bees and honey bees are chasing each other over the gold door of the moon and up over the silver transoms."

116

Dippy the Wisp took out a bee-bag, took bees out of the bee-bag, balanced the bees on her thumb, humming a humpty dumpty song. And Slip Me Liz, looking on, joined in on the humpty dumpty song. And, of course, the bees began buzzing and buzzing their *bee* humpty dumpty song.

"Have you fastened names on them?" asked the Potato Face.

"These three on my thumb, these three special blue-violet bees, I put their names on silk white ribbons and tied the ribbons to their knees. This is Egypt—she has inkwells in her ears. This is Jesse James—he puts postage stamps on his nose. This is Spanish Onions—she likes pearl-color handkerchiefs around her yellow neck."

"Bees belong in bee-bags, but these are different," the old man murmured.

"Runaway bees, these are," Dippy the Wisp went on. "They buzz away, they come buzzing back, buzzing home, buzzing secrets, syllables, snitches.

"To-day Egypt came buzzing home with her inkwells in her ears. And Egypt buzzed, 'I flew and flew and I buzzed and buzzed far, far away, till I came where I met the Queen of the Cracked Heads with her head all cracked. And she took me by the foot and took me to the palace of the Cracked Heads with their heads all cracked.

" 'The palace was full of goats walking up and down the stairs, sliding on the banisters eating bingety bing clocks. Before he bites the clock and chews and swallows and eats the bingety bing clock, I noticed, each goat winds up the clock and fixes it to go off bling bling bingety bing, after he eats it down. I noticed that. And the fat, fat, puffy goats, the fat, fat, waddly goats, had extra clocks hung on their horns—and the clocks, tired of waiting, spoke to each other in the bingety bing clock talk. I noticed that too.

She was sitting on a ladder feeding baby clocks to
the baby alligators

" 'I stayed all morning and I saw them feed the big goats big hunks and the little goats little hunks and the big clocks big bings and the little clocks little bings. At last in the afternoon, the queen of the Cracked Heads came with her cracked head to say good-by to me. She was sitting on a ladder feeding baby clocks to baby alligators, winding the clocks and fixing the bingety bings, so after the baby alligators swallowed the clocks, I heard them singing bling bling bingety bing.

" 'And the Queen was reading the alphabet to the littlest of the baby alligators—and they were saying the alligator A B C while she was saying the A B C of the Cracked Heads. At last she said good-by to me, good-by and come again soon, good-by and stay longer next time.'

" 'When I went out of the door all the baby alligators climbed up the ladder and bingety blinged good-by to me. I buzzed home fast because I was lonesome. I am so, *so* glad to be home again.' "

The Potato Face looked up and said, "This is nice as the rats on the moon in the middle of the winter locking their mittens in the ice box. Tell us next about that blue-violet bumblebee, Jesse James."

"Jesse James," said Dippy the Wisp, "Jesse James came buzzing home with a postage stamp on his nose. And Jesse James buzzed, 'I flew and I flew and buzzed and buzzed far, far away till I came where I met the King of the Paper Sacks who lives in a palace of paper sacks. I went inside the palace expecting to see paper sacks everywhere. But instead of paper sacks the palace was full of pink and purple peanuts walking up and down the stairs washing their faces, stitching handkerchiefs.'

" 'In the evening all the pink and purple peanuts put on their overshoes and make paper sacks. The King of the Paper Sacks walks around and around among them saying, "If

122

anybody asks you who I am tell them I am the King of the Paper Sacks." And one little peanut flipped up one time in the King's face and asked, "Say it again—*who* do you think you are?" And it made the King so bitter in his feelings he reached out his hand and with a sweep and a swoop he swept fifty pink and purple peanuts into a paper sack and cried out, "A nickel a sack, a nickel a sack." And he threw them into a trash pile of tin cans.

" 'When I went away he shook hands with me and said, "Good-by, Jesse James, you old buzzer, if anybody asks you tell them you saw the King of the Paper Sacks where he lives.

" 'When I went away from the palace, the doors and the window sills, the corners of the roofs and the eave troughs where the rain runs off, they were all full of pink and purple peanuts standing in their overshoes washing their faces, stitching handkerchiefs, calling good-by to me, good-by and come again, good-by and

123

stay longer next time. Then I came buzzing home because I was lonesome. And I am so, *so* glad to be home again.' "

The Potato Face looked up again and said, "It *is* a misty moisty evening in the moonshine. Now tell us about that blue-violet honeybee, Spanish Onions."

And Dippy the Wisp tied a slipknot in the pearl-color handkerchief around the yellow neck of Spanish Onions and said, "Spanish Onions came buzzing back home with her face dirty and scared and she told us, 'I flew and flew and I buzzed and buzzed till I came where I met the Queen of the Empty Hats. She took me by the foot and took me across the City of the Empty Hats, saying under her breath, "There is a screw loose somewhere, there is a leak in the tank." Fat rats, fat bats, fat cats, came along under empty hats and the Queen always said under her breath, "There is a screw loose somewhere, there is a leak in the tank." In the houses, on the street, riding on the rattlers and the razz cars, the only people were hats, empty hats. When the fat rats changed hats with the fat bats, the hats were empty. When the fat bats changed *those* hats with the fat cats, the hats were empty. I took off my hat and saw it was empty. *I began to feel like an empty hat myself.* I got scared. I jumped loose from the Queen of the Empty Hats and buzzed back home fast. I am so, *so* glad to be home again.' "

The Potato Face sat hugging his accordion. He looked up and said, "Put the bees back in the bee-bag—they buzz too many secrets, syllables and snitches."

"What do you expect when the moon is a gold door with silver transoms?" asked Slip Me Liz.

"Yes," said Dippy the Wisp. "What do you expect when the bumblebees and the honeybees are chasing each other over the gold door of the moon and up over the silver transoms?"

125

And the two tough pony girls, the two limber prairie girls, went away humming a little humpty dumpty song across the moonshine gold on the tops of the rainpools.

How Hot Balloons and His Pigeon Daughters Crossed Over into the Rootabaga Country

Hot Balloons was a man who lived all alone among people who sell slips, flips, flicks and chicks by the dozen, by the box, by the box car job lot, back and forth to each other.

Hot Balloons used to open the window in the morning and say to the rag pickers and the rag handlers, "Far, far away the pigeons are calling; far, far away the white wings are dipping in the blue, in the sky blue."

And the rag pickers and the rag handlers looked up from their rag bags and said, "Far, far away the rags are flying; far, far away the rags are whistling in the wind, in the sky wind."

Now two pigeons came walking up to the door, the door knob and the door bell under the window of Hot Balloons. One of the pigeons rang the bell. The other pigeon, too, stepped up to the bell and gave it a ring.

Then they waited, tying the shoe strings on their shoes and the bonnet strings under their chins, while they waited.

Hot Balloons opened the door. And they flew into his hands, one pigeon apiece in each of his hands, flipping and fluttering their wings, calling, "Ka loo, ka loo, ka lo, ka lo," leaving a letter in his hands and then flying away fast.

Hot Balloons stepped out on the front steps to read the letter where the light was good in

One of the pigeons rang the bell

the daylight because it was so early in the morning. The letter was on paper scribbled over in pigeon foot blue handwriting with many secrets and syllables.

After Hot Balloons read the letter, he said to himself, "I wonder if those two pigeons are my two runaway daughters, Dippy the Wisp and Slip Me Liz. When they ran away they said they would cross the Shampoo river and go away into the Rootabaga country to live. And I have heard it is a law of the Rootabaga country whenever a girl crosses the Shampoo river to come back where she used to be, she changes into a pigeon—and she stays a pigeon till she crosses back over the Shampoo river into the Rootabaga country again."

And he shaded his eyes with his hands and looked far, far away in the blue, in the sky blue. And by looking long and hard he saw far, far away in the sky blue, the two white pigeons dipping their wings in the blue, flying fast, circling and circling higher and higher, toward the Shampoo river, toward the Rootabaga country.

"I wonder, I guess, I think so," he said to himself, "I wonder, I think so, it must be those two pigeons are my two runaway daughters, my two girls, Dippy the Wisp and Slip Me Liz."

He took out the letter and read it again right side up, upside down, back and forth. "It is the first time I ever read pigeon foot blue handwriting," he said to himself. And the way he read the letter, it said to him:

Daddy, daddy, daddy, come home to us in the Rootabaga country where the pigeons call ka loo, ka loo, ka lo, ka lo, where the squirrels carry ladders and the wildcats ask riddles and the fish jump out of the rivers and speak to the frying pans, where the baboons take care of the babies and the black cats come and go in orange and gold stockings, where the birds wear rose and purple hats on Monday afternoons up in the skylights in the evening.

(Signed) DIPPY THE WISP,
SLIP ME LIZ.

And reading the letter a second time, Hot Balloons said to himself, "No wonder it is scribbled over the paper in pigeon foot blue handwriting. No wonder it is full of secrets and syllables."

So he jumped into a shirt and a necktie, he jumped into a hat and a vest, and he jumped into a steel car, starting with a snizz and a snoof till it began running smooth and even as a catfoot.

"I will ride to the Shampoo river faster than two pigeons fly," he said. "I will be there."

Which he was. He got there before the two pigeons. But it was no use. For the rain and the rainstorm was working—and the rain and the rainstorm tore down and took and washed away the steel bridge over the Shampoo river.

"Now there is only an air bridge to cross on, and a *steel* car drops down, falls off, falls through, if it runs on an *air* bridge," he said.

So he was all alone with the rain and the rainstorm all around him—and far as he could see by shading his eyes and looking, there was only the rain and the rainstorm across the river —and the *air* bridge.

While he waited for the rain and the rainstorm to go down, two pigeons came flying into his hands, one apiece into each hand, flipping and fluttering their wings and calling, "Ka loo, ka loo, ka lo, ka lo." And he could tell by the way they began tying the shoestrings on their shoes and the bonnet strings under their chins, they were the same two pigeons ringing the door bell that morning.

They wrote on his thumb-nails in pigeon foot blue handwriting, and he read their handwriting asking him why he didn't cross over the Shampoo river. And he explained, "There is only an *air* bridge to cross on. A *steel* car drops down, falls off, falls through, if it runs on an *air* bridge. Change my *steel* car to an *air* car. Then I can cross the *air* bridge."

The pigeons flipped and fluttered, dipped their wings and called, "Ka loo, ka loo, ka lo, ka lo." And they scribbled their pigeon feet on his thumb-nail—telling him to wait. So the pigeons went flying across the Shampoo river.

They came back with a basket. In the basket was a snoox and a gringo. And the snoox and the gringo took hammers, jacks, flanges, nuts, screws, bearings, ball bearings, axles, axle grease, ax handles, spits, spitters, spitballs and spitfires, and worked.

"It's a hot job," said the snoox to the gringo. "I'll say it's a hot job," said the gringo answering the snoox.

"We'll give this one the merry razoo," said the snoox to the gringo, working overtime and double time. "Yes, we'll put her to the cleaners and shoot her into high," said the gringo, answering the snoox, working overtime and double time.

They changed the steel to air, made an *air*

car out of the *steel* car, put Hot Balloons and the two pigeons into the air car and *drove the air car across the air bridge.*

And nowadays when people talk about it in the Rootabaga country, they say, "The snoox and the gringo drove the air car across the air bridge clean and cool as a whistle in the wind. As soon as the car got off the bridge and over into the Rootabaga country, the two pigeons changed in a flash. And Hot Balloons saw they were his two daughters, his two runaway girls, Dippy the Wisp and Slip Me Liz, standing and smiling at him and looking fresh and free as two fresh fish in a free river, fresh and free as two fresh bimbos in a bamboo tree.

He kissed them both, two long kisses, and while he was kissing them the snoox and the gringo worked double time and overtime and changed the *air* car back into a *steel* car.

And Dippy the Wisp and Slip Me Liz rode in that car—starting with a snizz and a snoof till it began running smooth and even as a catfoot—showing their father, Hot Balloons, where the squirrels carry ladders and the wild-cats ask riddles and the fish jump out of the rivers and speak to the frying pans, where the baboons take care of the babies and the black cats come and go in orange and gold stockings, where the birds wear rose and purple hats on Monday afternoons up in the skylights in the evening.

And often on a Saturday night or a New Year Eve or a Christmas morning, Hot Balloons remembers back how things used to be, and he tells his two girls about the rag pickers and the rag handlers back among the people who sell slips, flips, flicks, and chicks, by the dozen, by the box, by the box car job lot, back and forth to each other.

How Two Sweetheart Dippies Sat in the Moonlight on a Lumber Yard Fence and Heard About the Sooners and the Boomers

Not so very far and not so very near the Village of Liver-and-Onions is a dippy little town where dippy people used to live.

And it was long, long ago the sweetheart dippies stood in their windows and watched the dips of the star dippers in the dip of the sky.

It was the dippies who took the running wild oleander and the cunning wild rambler rose and kept them so the running wild winters let them alone.

"It is easy to be a dippy . . . among the dippies . . . isn't it?" the sweetheart dippies whispered to each other, sitting in the leaf shadows of the oleander, the rambler rose.

The name of this dippy town came by accident. The name of the town is Thumbs Up and it used to be named Thumbs Down and expects to change its name back and forth between Thumbs Up and Thumbs Down.

The running wild oleanders and the running wild rambler roses grow there over the big lumber yards where all the old lumber goes.

The dippies and the dippy sweethearts go out there to those lumber yards and sit on the fence moonlight nights and look at the lumber.

The rusty nails in the lumber get rustier and rustier till they drop out. And whenever they drop out there is always a rat standing under to take the nail in his teeth and chew the nail and eat it.

For this is the place the nail-eating rats come to from all over the Rootabaga country. Father rats and mother rats send the young rats there to eat nails and get stronger.

If a young rat comes back from a trip to the lumber yards in Thumbs Up and he meets another young rat going to those lumber yards, they say to each other, "Where have you been?" "To Thumbs Up." "And how do you feel?" *"Hard as nails."*

Now one night two of the dippies, a sweetheart boy and girl, went out to the big lumber yards and sat on the fence and looked at the lumber and the running wild oleanders and the running wild rambler roses.

And they saw two big rusty nails, getting rustier and rustier, drop out of the lumber and drop into the teeth of two young rats.

And the two young rats sat up on their tails there in the moonlight under the oleanders, under the roses, and one of the young rats told the other young rat a story he made up out of his head.

Chewing on the big rusty nail and then swallowing, telling more of the story after swallowing and before beginning to chew the nail again, this is the story he told—and this is the story the two dippies, the two sweethearts sitting on the fence in the moonlight, heard:

Far away where the sky drops down, and the sunsets open doors for the nights to come through—where the running winds meet, change faces and come back—there is a prairie where the green grass grows all around.

And on that prairie the gophers, the black and brown-striped ground squirrels, sit with their backs straight up, sitting on their soft paddy tails, sitting in the spring song murmur of the south wind, saying to each other, "This is the prairie and the prairie belongs to us."

Heard About Sooners and Boomers

Now far back in the long time, the gophers came there, chasing each other, playing the-green-grass-grew-all-around, playing cross tag, hop tag, skip tag, billy-be-tag, billy-be-it.

The razorback hogs came then, eating pig-nuts, potatoes, paw paws, pumpkins. The wild horse, the buffalo, came. The moose, with spraggly branches of antlers spreading out over his head, the moose came—and the fox, the wolf.

The gophers flipped a quick flip-flop back into their gopher holes when the fox, the wolf, came. And the fox, the wolf, stood at the holes and said, "You *look* like rats, you *run* like rats, you *are* rats, rats with stripes. Bah! you are only *rats*. Bah!"

It was the first time anybody said "Bah!" to the gophers. They sat in a circle with their noses up asking, "*What* does this 'Bah!' mean?" And an old timer, with his hair falling off in patches, with the stripes on his soft paddy tail patched with patches, this old timer of a gopher said, " 'Bah!' speaks more than it means whenever it is spoken."

Then the sooners and the boomers came, saying "Bah!" and saying it many new ways, till the fox, the wolf, the moose, the wild horse, the buffalo, the razorback hog picked up their feet and ran away without looking back.

The sooners and boomers began making houses, sod houses, log, lumber, plaster-and-lath houses, stone, brick, steel houses, but most of the houses were lumber with nails to hold the lumber together to keep the rain off and push the wind back and hold the blizzards outside.

In the beginning the sooners and boomers told stories, spoke jokes, made songs, with their arms on each other's shoulders. They dug wells, helping each other get water. They built chimneys together helping each other let the smoke out of their houses. And every year the day before Thanksgiving they went in

144

cahoots with their post hole diggers and dug all the post holes for a year to come. That was in the morning. In the afternoon they took each other's cistern cleaners and cleaned all the cisterns for a year to come. And the next day on Thanksgiving they split turkey wishbones and thanked each other they had all the post holes dug and all the cisterns cleaned for a year to come.

If the boomers had to have broom corn to make brooms the sooners came saying, "Here is your broom corn." If the sooners had to have a gallon of molasses, the boomers came saying, "Here is your gallon of molasses."

They handed each other big duck eggs to fry, big goose eggs to boil, purple pigeon eggs for Easter breakfast. Wagon loads of buff banty eggs went back and forth between the sooners and boomers. And they took big hayracks full of buff banty hens and traded them for hayracks full of buff banty roosters.

And one time at a picnic, one summer afternoon, the sooners gave the boomers a thousand golden ice tongs with hearts and hands carved on the handles. And the boomers gave the sooners a thousand silver wheelbarrows with hearts and hands carved on the handles.

Then came pigs, pigs, pigs, and more pigs. And the sooners and boomers said the pigs had to be painted. There was a war to decide whether the pigs should be painted pink or green. Pink won.

The next war was to decide whether the pigs should be painted checks or stripes. Checks won. The next war after that was to decide whether the checks should be painted pink or green. Green won.

Then came the longest war of all, up till that time. And this war decided the pigs should be painted both pink and green, both checks and stripes.

They rested then. But it was only a short rest. For then came the war to decide whether peach pickers must pick peaches on Tuesday mornings or on Saturday afternoons. Tuesday mornings won. This was a short war. Then came a long war—to decide whether telegraph pole climbers must eat onions at noon with spoons, or whether dishwashers must keep their money in pig's ears with padlocks pinched on with pincers.

So the wars went on. Between wars they called each other goofs and snoofs, grave robbers, pickpockets, porch climbers, pie thieves, pie face mutts, bums, big bums, big greasy bums, dummies, mummies, rummies, sneezicks, bohunks, wops, snorkies, ditch diggers, peanuts, fatheads, sapheads, pinheads, pickle faces, horse thieves, rubbernecks, big pieces of cheese, big bags of wind, snabs, scabs, and dirty sniveling snitches. Sometimes when they got tired of calling each other names they scratched in the air with their fingers and made faces with their tongues out twisted like pretzels.

After a while, it seemed, there was no corn, no broom corn, no brooms, not even teeny sweepings of corn or broom corn or brooms. And there were no duck eggs to fry, goose eggs to boil, no buff banty eggs, no buff banty hens, no buff banty roosters, no wagons for wagon loads of buff banty eggs, no hayracks for hayrack loads of buff banty hens and buff banty roosters.

And the thousand golden ice tongs the sooners gave the boomers, and the thousand silver wheelbarrows the boomers gave the sooners, both with hearts and hands carved on the handles, they were long ago broken up in one of the early wars deciding pigs must be painted both pink and green with both checks and stripes.

And now, at last, there were no more pigs to paint either pink or green or with checks or stripes. The pigs, pigs, pigs, were gone.

So the sooners and boomers all got lost in the wars or they screwed wooden legs on their stump legs and walked away to bigger, bigger prairies or they started away for the rivers and mountains, stopping always to count how many fleas there were in any bunch of fleas they met. If you see anybody who stops to count the fleas in a bunch of fleas, that is a sign he is either a sooner or a boomer.

So again the gophers, the black and brown striped ground squirrels, sit with their backs straight up, sitting on their soft paddy tails, sitting in the spring song murmur of the south wind, saying, "This is the prairie and the prairie belongs to us."

Far away to-day where the sky drops down and the sunsets open doors for the nights to come through—where the running winds meet, change faces and come back—there the gophers are playing the-green-grass-grew-all-around, playing cross tag, skip tag, hop tag, billy-be-tag, billy-be-it. And sometimes they sit in a circle and ask, "What does this 'Bah!' mean?" And an old timer answers, " 'Bah!' speaks more than it means whenever it is spoken."

Two Sweetheart Dippies

That was the story the young rat under the oleanders, under the roses, told the other young rat, while the two sweetheart dippies sat on the fence in the moonlight looking at the lumber and listening.

The young rat who told the story hardly got started eating the nail he was chewing, while the young rat that did the listening chewed up and swallowed down a whole nail.

As the two dippies on the fence looked at the running wild oleander and the running wild rambler roses over the lumber in the moonlight, they said to each other, "It's easy to be a dippy . . . among the dippies . . . isn't it?" And they climbed down from the fence and went home in the moonlight.

7. Two Stories Out of the Tall Grass.

People: John Jack Johannes Humma-
dummaduffer
Feed Box
Eva Evelyn Evangeline Hum-
madummaduffer
Sky Blue
The Harvest Moon
A Haystack Cricket

Baby Moon
Half Moon
Silver Moon

Doorbells, Chimneys, Cellars

The Night Policeman in the
Village of Cream Puffs
Butter Fingers
Three Strikes
Cub Ballplayers

The Haystack Cricket and How Things Are Different Up in the Moon Towns

There is an old man with wrinkles like wrinkled leather on his face living among the cornfields on the rolling prairie near the Shampoo river.

His name is John Jack Johannes Hummadummaduffer. His cronies and the people who know him call him Feed Box.

His daughter is a cornfield girl with hair

153

shining the way cornsilk shines when the corn is ripe in the fall time. The tassels of cornsilk hang down and blow in the wind with a rusty dark gold, and they seem to get mixed with her hair. Her name is Eva Evelyn Evangeline Hummadummaduffer. And her chums and the people who know her call her Sky Blue.

The eleventh month, November, comes every year to the corn belt on that rolling prairie. The wagons bring the corn from the fields in the harvest days and the cracks in the corncribs shine with the yellow and gold of the corn.

The harvest moon comes, too. They say it stacks sheaves of the November gold moonshine into gold corn shocks on the sky. So they say.

On those mornings in November that time of the year, the old man they call Feed Box sits where the sun shines against the boards of a corncrib.

The girl they call Sky Blue, even though her name is Eva Evelyn Evangeline Hummadummaduffer, she comes along one November morning. Her father is sitting in the sun with his back against a corncrib. And he tells her he always sits there every year listening to the mice in the cornfields getting ready to move into the big farmhouse.

"When the frost comes and the corn is husked and put in the corncribs, the fields are cleaned and the cold nights come. Papa mouse and mama mouse tell the little ones it is time to sneak into the cellar and the garret and the attic of the farmhouse," said Feed Box to Sky Blue.

"I am listening," she said, "and I can hear the papa mouse and the mama mouse telling the little ones how they will find rags and paper and wool and splinters and shavings and hair, and they will make warm nests for the winter in the big farmhouse—if no kits, cats nor kittycats get them."

155

The Haystack Cricket and How Things

The old man, Feed Box, rubbed his back and his shoulders against the boards of the corncrib and washed his hands almost as if he might be washing them in the gold of the autumn sunshine. Then he told this happening:

This time of the year, when the mouse in the fields whispers so I can hear him, I remember one November when I was a boy.

One night in November when the harvest moon was shining and stacking gold cornshocks in the sky, I got lost. Instead of going home I was going away from home. And the next day and the next night instead of going home I was going away from home.

That second night I came to a haystack where a yellow and gold cricket was singing. And he was singing the same songs the crickets sing in the haystacks back home where the Hummadummaduffers raise hay and corn, in the corn belt near the Shampoo river.

And he told me, this cricket did, he told me when he listened soft if everything was still in the grass and the sky, he could hear golden crickets singing in the cornshocks the harvest moon had stacked in the sky.

I went to sleep listening to the singing of the yellow and gold crickets in that haystack. It was early in the morning, long before daylight, I guess, the two of us went on a trip away from the haystack.

We took a trip. The yellow and gold cricket led the way. "It is the call of the harvest moon," he said to me in a singing whisper. "We are going up to the moon towns where the harvest moon stacks the cornshocks on the sky."

We came to a little valley in the sky. And the harvest moon had slipped three little towns into that valley, three little towns named Half Moon, Baby Moon, and Silver Moon.

In the town of Half Moon they *look* out of the doors and *come in* at the windows. So they have taken all the doorbells off the doors and put them on the windows. Whenever we rang a doorbell we went to a window.

In the town of Baby Moon they had windows on the chimneys so the smoke can look out of the window and see the weather before it comes out over the top of the chimney. And whenever the chimneys get tired of being stuck up on the top of the roof, the chimneys climb down and dance in the cellar. We saw five chimneys climb down and join hands and bump heads and dance a laughing chimney dance.

In the town of Silver Moon the cellars are not satisfied. They say to each other, "We are tired of being under, always under." So the cellars slip out from being under, always under. They slip out and climb up on top of the roof.

And that was all we saw up among the moon towns of Half Moon, Baby Moon and Silver Moon. We had to get back to the haystack so as to get up in the morning after our night sleep.

"This time of the year I always remember that November," said the old man, Feed Box, to his daughter, Sky Blue.

And Sky Blue said, "I am going to sleep in a haystack sometime in November just to see if a yellow and gold cricket will come with a singing whisper and take me on a trip to where the doorbells are on the windows and the chimneys climb down and dance."

The old man murmured, "Don't forget the cellars tired of being under, always under."

Why the Big Ball Game Between Hot Grounders and the Grand Standers Was a Hot Game

Up near the Village of Cream Puffs is a string of ball towns hiding in the tall grass. Passengers in the railroad trains look out of the windows and the tall grass stands up so they can't see the ball towns. But the ball towns are there and the tall grass is full of pitchers, catchers, basemen, fielders, short stops, sluggers, southpaws and backstops. They play

161

ball till dark and after dark they talk ball. The big fast ballplayers in the Rootabaga Country all come from these ball towns in the tall grass.

The towns used to have names like names in books. But now the names are all like ball talk: Knock the Cover Off, Home Plate, Chest Protector, Grand Stand, Nine Innings, Three Balls and Two Strikes, Bases Full and Two Out, Big League, Bush League, Hot Grounder, Out Drop, Bee Liner, Muffs and Pick Ups, Slide Kelly Slide, Paste It On the Nose.

Now the Night Policeman in the Village of Cream Puffs stopped in at the Cigar Store one night and a gang of cub ballplayers loafing and talking ball talk asked him if there was anything in the wind. And he told them this happening:

"I was sitting on the front steps of the postoffice last night thinking how many letters get lost and how many letters never get answered. A ballplayer came along with a package and said his name was Butter Fingers and he was the heavy hitter, the hard slugger, for the Grand Stand ball team playing a championship game the day before with the Hot Grounders ball team. He came to the Village of Cream Puffs the day before the game, found a snoox and a gringo and got the snoox and the gringo to make him *a home run shirt*. Wearing a home run shirt, he told me, you knock a home run every time you come to bat. He said he knocked a home run every time he came to bat, and it was his home runs won the game for the Grand Standers. He was carrying a package and said the home run shirt was in the package and he was taking it back to the snoox and the gringo because he promised he wouldn't keep it, and it belonged to the snoox and the gringo and they only rented it to him for the championship game. The last I saw of him he was hot-footing it pitty-pat pitty-pat up the street with the package.

"Well, I just said tra-la-loo to Butter Fingers when along comes another ballplayer. He had a package too, and he said his name was Three Strikes, and he was the left-handed southpaw pitcher for the Hot Grounders team the day before playing a game against the Grand Stand team. He said he knew unless he put over some classy pitching the game was lost and everything was goose eggs. So he came to the Village of Cream Puffs the day before the game, found a snoox and a gringo and got the snoox and the gringo to make him *a spitball shirt*. A spitball looks easy, he told me, but it has smoke and whiskers and nobody can touch it. He said he handed the Grand Standers a line of inshoots close to their chins and they never got to first base. Three Strikes was carrying a package and he said the spitball shirt was in the package, and he was taking it back to the snoox and the gringo because he promised he wouldn't keep it and it belonged to the snoox and the gringo and they only rented it to him. The last I saw of him he was hot-footing it pitty-pat pitty-pat up the street with a package."

The gang of cub ballplayers in the Cigar Store asked the Night Policeman, "Who won the game? Was it the Grand Standers or the Hot Grounders took the gravvy?"

"You can search me for the answer," he told the boys. "If the snoox and the gringo come past the postoffice to-night when I sit on the front steps wondering how so many letters get lost and how so many never get answered, I will ask the snoox and the gringo and if they tell me to-night I'll tell you to-morrow night."

And ever since then when they talk ball talk in the ball towns hiding in the tall grass they

165

say the only sure way to win a ball game is to have a pitcher with a spitball shirt and over that a home run shirt, both made by a snoox and a gringo.

8. Two Stories Out of Oklahoma and Nebraska.

People: Jonas Jonas Huckabuck
Mama Mama Huckabuck
Pony Pony Huckabuck

A Yellow Squash
A Silver Buckle
A Chinese Silver Slipper
    Buckle
Pop Corn

Yang Yang
Hoo Hoo
Their Mother

The Shadow of the Goose
The Left Foot of the
    Shadow of the Goose
An Oklahoma Home

The Huckabuck Family and How They Raised Pop Corn in Nebraska and Quit and Came Back

Jonas Jonas Huckabuck was a farmer in Nebraska with a wife, Mama Mama Huckabuck, and a daughter, Pony Pony Huckabuck.

"Your father gave you two names the same in front," people had said to him.

And he answered, "Yes, two names are easier to remember. If you call me by my first name Jonas and I don't hear you then when you call me by my second name Jonas maybe I will.

"And," he went on, "I call my pony-face girl Pony Pony because if she doesn't hear me the first time she always does the second."

And so they lived on a farm where they raised pop corn, these three, Jonas Jonas Huckabuck, his wife, Mama Mama Huckabuck, and their pony-face daughter, Pony Pony Huckabuck.

After they harvested the crop one year they had the barns, the cribs, the sheds, the shacks, and all the cracks and corners of the farm, all filled with pop corn.

"We came out to Nebraska to raise pop corn," said Jonas Jonas, "and I guess we got nearly enough pop corn this year for the pop corn poppers and all the friends and relations of all the pop corn poppers in these United States."

And this was the year Pony Pony was going to bake her first squash pie all by herself. In

170

She carried the squash into the kitchen

one corner of the corn crib, all covered over with pop corn, she had a secret, a big round squash, a fat yellow squash, a rich squash all spotted with spots of gold.

She carried the squash into the kitchen, took a long sharp shining knife, and then she cut the squash in the middle till she had two big half squashes. And inside just like outside it was rich yellow spotted with spots of gold.

And there was a shine of silver. And Pony Pony wondered why silver should be in a squash. She picked and plunged with her fingers till she pulled it out.

"It's a buckle," she said, " a silver buckle, a Chinese silver slipper buckle."

She ran with it to her father and said, "Look what I found when I cut open the golden yellow squash spotted with gold spots —it is a Chinese silver slipper buckle."

"It means our luck is going to change, and we don't know whether it will be good luck or bad luck," said Jonas Jonas to his daughter, Pony Pony Huckabuck.

Then she ran with it to her mother and said, "Look what I found when I cut open the yellow squash spotted with spots of gold—it is a Chinese silver slipper buckle."

"It means our luck is going to change, and we don't know whether it will be good luck or bad luck," said Mama Mama Huckabuck.

And that night a fire started in the barns, crib, sheds, shacks, cracks, and corners, where the pop corn harvest was kept. All night long the pop corn popped. In the morning the ground all around the farm house and the barn was covered with white pop corn so it looked like a heavy fall of snow.

All the next day the fire kept on and the pop corn popped till it was up to the shoulders of Pony Pony when she tried to walk from the house to the barn. And that night in all the barns, cribs, sheds, shacks, cracks and corners of the farm, the pop corn went on popping.

In the morning when Jonas Jonas Huckabuck looked out of the upstairs window he saw the pop corn popping and coming higher and higher. It was nearly up to the window. Before evening and dark of that day, Jonas Jonas Huckabuck, and his wife Mama Mama Huckabuck, and their daughter Pony Pony Huckabuck, all went away from the farm saying, "We came to Nebraska to raise pop corn, but this is too much. We will not come back till the wind blows away the pop corn. We will not come back till we get a sign and a signal."

They went to Oskaloosa, Iowa. And the next year Pony Pony Huckabuck was very proud because when she stood on the sidewalks in the street she could see her father sitting high on the seat of a coal wagon, driving two big spanking horses hitched with shining brass harness in front of the coal wagon. And though Pony Pony and Jonas Jonas were proud, very proud all that year, there never came a sign, a signal.

The next year again was a proud year, exactly as proud a year as they spent in Oskaloosa. They went to Paducah, Kentucky, to Defiance, Ohio; Peoria, Illinois; Indianapolis, Indiana; Walla Walla, Washington. And in all these places Pony Pony Huckabuck saw her father, Jonas Jonas Huckabuck, standing in rubber boots deep down in a ditch with a shining steel shovel shoveling yellow clay and black mud from down in the ditch high and high up over his shoulders. And though it was a proud year they got no sign, no signal.

The next year came. It was the proudest of all. This was the year Jonas Jonas Huckabuck and his family lived in Elgin, Illinois, and Jonas Jonas was watchman in a watch factory watching the watches.

"I know where you have been," Mama Mama Huckabuck would say of an evening to

Pony Pony Huckabuck. "You have been down to the watch factory watching your father watch the watches."

"Yes," said Pony Pony. "Yes, and this evening when I was watching father watch the watches in the watch factory, I looked over my left shoulder and I saw a policeman with a star and brass buttons and he was watching me to see if I was watching father watch the watches in the watch factory."

It was a proud year. Pony Pony saved her money. Thanksgiving came. Pony Pony said, "I am going to get a squash to make a squash pie." She hunted from one grocery to another; she kept her eyes on the farm wagons coming into Elgin with squashes.

She found what she wanted, the yellow squash spotted with gold spots. She took it home, cut it open, and saw the inside was like the outside, all rich yellow spotted with gold spots.

There was a shine like silver. She picked

177

and plunged with her fingers and pulled and pulled till at last she pulled out the shine of silver.

"It's a sign; it is a signal," she said. "It is a buckle, a slipper buckle, a Chinese silver slipper buckle. It is the mate to the other buckle. Our luck is going to change. Yoo hoo! Yoo hoo!"

She told her father and mother about the buckle. They went back to the farm in Nebraska. The wind by this time had been blowing and blowing for three years, and all the pop corn was blown away.

"Now we are going to be farmers again," said Jonas Jonas Huckabuck to Mama Mama Huckabuck and to Pony Pony Huckabuck. "And we are going to raise cabbages, beets and turnips; we are going to raise squash, rutabaga, pumpkins and peppers for pickling. We are going to raise wheat, oats, barley, rye. We are going to raise corn such as Indian corn and kaffir corn—but we are *not* going to raise any pop corn for the pop corn poppers to be popping."

And the pony-face daughter, Pony Pony Huckabuck, was proud because she had on new black slippers, and around her ankles, holding the slippers on the left foot and the right foot, she had two buckles, silver buckles, Chinese silver slipper buckles. They were mates.

Sometimes on Thanksgiving Day and Chrismas and New Year's, she tells her friends to be careful when they open a squash.

"Squashes make your luck change good to bad and bad to good," says Pony Pony.

Yang Yang and Hoo Hoo, or the Song of the Left Foot of the Shadow of the Goose in Oklahoma

Yang Yang and Hoo Hoo were two girls who used to live in Battle Ax, Michigan, before they moved to Wagon Wheel Gap, Colorado, and back to Broken Doors, Ohio, and then over to Open Windows, Iowa, and at last down to Alfafa Clover, Oklahoma, where they say, "Our Oklahoma home is in Oklahoma."

One summer morning Yang Yang and Hoo

Hoo woke up saying to each other, "Our Oklahoma home is in Oklahoma." And it was that morning the shadow of a goose flew in at the open window, just over the bed where Yang Yang and Hoo Hoo slept with their eyes shut all night and woke with their eyes open in the morning.

The shadow of the goose fluttered a while along the ceiling, flickered a while along the wall, and then after one more flutter and flicker put itself on the wall like a picture of a goose put there to look at, only it was a living picture—and it made its neck stretch in a curve and then stretch straight.

"Yang yang," cried Yang Yang. "Yang yang."

"Hoo hoo," sang Hoo Hoo. "Hoo hoo."

And while Hoo Hoo kept on calling a soft, low coaxing hoo hoo, Yang Yang kept on crying a hard, noisy nagging yang yang till everybody in the house upstairs and down and everybody in the neighbor houses heard her yang-yanging.

The shadow of the goose lifted its left wing a little, lifted its right foot a little, got up on its goose legs, and walked around and around in a circle on its goose feet. And every time it walked around in a circle it came back to the same place it started from, with its left foot or right foot in the same foot spot it started from. Then it stayed there in the same place like a picture put there to look at, only it was a living picture with its neck sometimes sticking up straight in the air and sometimes bending in a long curving bend.

Yang Yang threw the bed covers off, slid out of bed and ran downstairs yang-yanging for her mother. But Hoo Hoo sat up in bed laughing, counting her pink toes to see if there were ten pink toes the same as the morning before. And while she was counting her pink toes she looked out of the corners of her eyes at the shadow of the goose on the wall.

183

And again the shadow of the goose lifted its left wing a little, lifted its right foot a little, got up on its goose legs, and walked around and around in a circle on its goose feet. And every time it walked around in a circle it came back to the same place it started from, with its left foot or right foot back in the same foot spot it started from. Then it stayed there in the same place where it put itself on the wall like a picture to look at, only it was a living picture with its neck sticking up straight in the air and then changing so its neck was bending in a long curving bend.

And all the time little Hoo Hoo was sitting up in bed counting her pink toes and looking out of the corners of her eyes at the shadow of the goose.

By and by little Hoo Hoo said, "Good morning—hoo hoo for you—and hoo hoo again, I was looking at the window when you came in. I saw you put yourself on the wall like a picture. I saw you begin to walk and come back where you started from with your neck sticking straight up and your neck bending in a bend. I give you good morning. I blow a hoo hoo to you. I blow two of a hoo hoo to you."

Then the shadow of a goose, as if to answer good morning, and as if to answer what Hoo Hoo meant by saying, "I blow two of a hoo hoo to you," stretched its neck sticking up straight and long, longer than any time yet, and then bended its neck in more of a bend than any time yet.

And all the time Hoo Hoo was sitting in bed feeling of her toes with her fingers to see if she had one toe for every finger, and to see if she had one pink little toe to match her one pink little finger, and to see if she had one fat flat big toe to match her one fat flat thumb.

Then when the room was all quiet the shadow of the goose lifted its left foot and began singing—singing just as the shadow of a goose always sings—with the left foot—very softly with the left foot—so softly you must listen with the softest little listeners you have deep inside your ears.

And this was the song, this was the old-time, old-fashioned left foot song the shadow of the goose sang for Hoo Hoo:

> Be a yang yang if you want to.
> Be a hoo hoo if you want to.
>
> The yang yangs always yang in the morning.
> The hoo hoos always hoo in the morning.
>
> Early in the morning the putters sit putting,
> Putting on your nose, putting on your ears,
> Putting in your eyes and the lashes on your eyes,
> Putting on the chins of your chinny chin chins.

And after singing the left foot song the shadow of the goose walked around in a long circle, came back where it started from, stopped and stood still with the proud stand-still of a goose, and then stretched its neck sticking up straight and long, longer than any time yet, and then bended its neck bent and twisted in longer bends than any time yet.

Then the shadow took itself off the wall, fluttered and flickered along the ceiling and over the bed, flew out of the window and was gone, leaving Hoo Hoo all alone sitting up in bed counting her pink toes.

Out of the corners of her eyes she looked up at the wall of the room, at the place where the shadow of the goose put itself like a picture. And there she saw a shadow spot. She looked and saw it was a left foot, the same left foot that had been singing the left foot song.

Soon Yang Yang came yang-yanging into the room holding to her mother's apron. Hoo Hoo told her mother all the happenings that happened. The mother wouldn't believe it. Then Hoo Hoo pointed up to the wall, to the left foot, the shadow spot left behind by the shadow of the goose when it took itself off the wall.

And now when Yang Yang and Hoo Hoo sleep all night with their eyes shut and wake up in the morning with their eyes open, sometimes they say, "Our Oklahoma home is in Oklahoma," and sometimes they sing:

Be a yang yang and yang yang if you want to.
Be a hoo hoo and hoo hoo if you want to.

9. One Story About Big People Now and Little People Long Ago.

People: Peter Potato Blossom Wishes
Three Whispering Cats
Hannah
Hannah More
Susquehannah

Hoom Slimmer

9. One Story About Big People Now and Little People Long Ago.

People: Peter Potato Blossom Wishes
Three Whispering Cats
Hannah
Hannah More
Susquehannah

Hoom Slimmer

How a Skyscraper and a Railroad Train Got Picked Up and Carried Away from Pig's Eye Valley Far in the Pickax Mountains

Peter Potato Blossom Wishes sat with her three cats, Hannah, Hannah More, and Susquehannah, one spring morning.

She was asking different kinds of questions of the three cats. But she always got the same answers no matter what she asked them.

They were whispering cats. Hannah was a yes-yes cat and always whispered yes-yes and nothing else. Hannah More was a no-no cat and always whispered no-no and nothing else. And Susquehannah was a stuttering cat and whispered halfway between yes and no, always hesitating and nothing else.

"The bye-low is whistling his bye-low and bye-low again," Peter said to herself with a murmur. "It is spring in the tall timbers and over the soft black lands. The hoo hoo and the biddywiddies come north to make a home again. The booblow blossoms put their cool white lips out into the blue mist. Every way I point my ears there is a bye-low whistling his bye-low and bye-low again. The spring in the timbers and black lands calls to the spring aching in my heart."

Now the three whispering cats heard what Peter Potato Blossom Wishes was murmuring to herself about the spring heartache.

And Hannah, the yes-yes cat, answered yes-yes. Hannah More, the no-no cat, answered no-no. And Susquehannah, the stuttering cat, hesitated halfway between yes-yes and no-no.

And Peter rubbed their fur the right way, scratched them softly between the ears, and murmured to herself, "It is a don't-care morning—I don't care."

And that morning her heart gave a hoist and a hist when she saw a speck of a blackbird spot far and high in the sky. Coming nearer it hummed, zoomed, hong whonged . . . shut off the hong whong . . . stoplocked and droplocked . . . and came down on the ground like a big easy bird with big wings stopped.

Hoom Slimmer slid out, wiped his hands on the oil rags, put a smear of axle grease on Peter's chin, kissed her on the nose, patted her ears two pats—and then they went into the house and had a late breakfast which was her second breakfast and his first.

"I flew till I came to Pig's Eye Valley in the Pickax Mountains," Hoom Slimmer told her. "The pickax pigs there run digging with their pickax feet and their pickax snouts. They are lean, long-legged pigs with pockets all over, fat pocket ears ahead and fat pocket tails behind, and the pockets full of rusty dust. They dip their noses in their pockets, sniff their noses full of rusty dust, and sneeze the rusty dust in each other's wrinkly, wriggly, wraggly faces.

"I took out a buzz shovel and scraper, pushed on the buzzer, and watched it dig and scrape out a city. The houses came to my ankles. The factories came to my knees. The top of the roof of the highest skyscraper came up to my nose.

"A spider ran out of a cellar. A book fell out of his mouth. It broke into rusty dust when I took hold of it. One page I saved. The reading on it said millions of people had read the book and millions more would read it."

Hoom Slimmer reached into a pocket. He took out in his hand a railroad train with an engine hooked on ahead, and a smoking car, coaches and sleeping cars hooked on behind.

"I cleaned it nice for you, Peter," he said.

"But the pickax pigs sneezed rusty dust on it. Put it in your handkerchief."

"And now," he went on, "I will wrap off the wrappers on the skyscraper. . . . Look at it! . . . It is thirty stories high. On top is a flagpole for a flag to go up. Halfway down is a clock, with the hands gone. On the first floor is a restaurant with signs, 'Watch Your Hats and Overcoats.' Here is the office of the building, with a sign on the wall, 'Be Brief.' Here the elevators ran up and down in a hurry. On doors are signs, bankers, doctors, lawyers, life insurance, fire insurance, steam hoist and operating engineers, bridge and structural iron and steel construction engineers, stocks, bonds, securities, architects, writers, detectives, window cleaners, jewelry, diamonds, cloaks, suits, shirts, sox, silk, wool, cotton, lumber, brick, sand, corn, oats, wheat, paper, ink, pencils, knives, guns, land, oil, coal, one door with a big sign, 'We Buy and Sell Anything,' another door, 'We Fix Anything,' and more doors, 'None Such,' 'The World's Finest,' 'The Best in the World,' 'Oldest Establishment in the World,' 'The World's Greatest,' 'None Greater,' 'Greatest in the World,' 'Greatest Ever Known.' "

And Hoom Slimmer put his arms around the skyscraper, lifted it on his shoulder, and carried it upstairs where Peter Potato Blossom said to put it, in a corner of her sleeping room. And she took out of her handkerchief the railroad train with the engine hooked on ahead and the smoking car, coaches and sleeping cars, hooked on behind. And she put the railroad train just next to the bottom floor of the skyscraper so people on the train could step off the train and step right into the skyscraper.

"Little railroad trains and little skyscrapers are just as big for little people as big railroad trains and big skyscrapers are for big people —is it not such?" she asked Hoom Slimmer.

And for an answer he gave her a looking glass half as long as her little finger and said,

196

"The women in that skyscraper used to look at themselves from head to foot in that looking glass."

Then Peter sang out like a spring bird song, "Now we are going to forget the pickax pigs sneezing rusty dust, and the Pig's Eye Valley and the Pickax Mountains. We are going out where the bye-low is whistling his bye-low and bye-low again, where it is spring in the tall timbers and over the soft black lands, where the hoo hoo and the biddywiddies come north to make a home again and the booblow blossoms put their cool white lips out into the blue mist."

And they sat under a tree where the early green of spring crooned in the black branches, and they could hear Hannah, Hannah More and Susquehannah, whispering yes-yes, no-no, and a hesitating stutter halfway between yes-yes, and no-no, always hesitating.

10. Three Stories About the Letter X and How It Got into the Alphabet.

> *People:* An Oyster King
> Shovel Ears
> Pig Wisps
> The Men Who Change the Alphabets
>
> A River Lumber King
> Kiss Me
> Flax Eyes
> Wildcats
>
> A Rich Man
> Blue Silver
> Her Playmates, Singing

There are six hundred different stories told in the Rootabaga Country about the first time the letter X got into the alphabet and how and why it was. The author has chosen three (3) of the shortest and strangest of those stories and they are told in the next and following pages.

Pig Wisps

There was an oyster king far in the south who knew how to open oysters and pick out the pearls.

He grew rich and all kinds of money came rolling in on him because he was a great oyster opener and knew how to pick out the pearls.

The son of this oyster king was named Shovel Ears. And it was hard for him to remember.

"He knows how to open oysters but he forgets to pick out the pearls," said the father of Shovel Ears.

Pig Wisps

"He is learning to remember worse and worse and to forget better and better," said the father of Shovel Ears.

Now in that same place far in the south was a little girl with two braids of hair twisted down her back and a face saying, "Here we come—where from?"

And her mother called her Pig Wisps.

Twice a week Pig Wisps ran to the butcher shop for a soup bone. Before starting she crossed her fingers and then the whole way to the butcher shop kept her fingers crossed.

If she met any playmates and they asked her to stop and play crosstag or jackstones or all-around-the-mulberry-bush or the-green-grass-grew-all-around or drop-the-handkerchief, she told them, "My fingers are crossed and I am running to the butcher shop for a soup bone."

One morning running to the butcher shop she bumped into a big queer boy and bumped him flat on the sidewalk.

"Did you look where you were running?" she asked him.

"I forgot again," said Shovel Ears. "I remember worse and worse. I forget better and better."

"Cross your fingers like this," said Pig Wisps, showing him how.

He ran to the butcher shop with her, watching her keep her fingers crossed till the butcher gave her the soup bone.

"After I get it then the soup bone reminds me to go home with it," she told him. "But until I get the soup bone I keep my fingers crossed."

Shovel Ears went to his father and began helping his father open oysters. And Shovel Ears kept his fingers crossed to remind him to pick out the pearls.

He picked a hundred buckets of pearls the first day and brought his father the longest slippery, shining rope of pearls ever seen in that oyster country.

"How do you do it?" his father asked.

"It is the crossed fingers—like this," said Shovel Ears, crossing his fingers like the letter X. "This is the way to remember better and forget worse."

It was then the oyster king went and told the men who change the alphabets just what happened.

When the men who change the alphabets heard just what happened, they decided to put in a new letter, the letter X, near the end of the alphabet, the sign of the crossed fingers.

On the wedding day of Pig Wisps and Shovel Ears, the men who change the alphabets all came to the wedding, with their fingers crossed.

Pig Wisps and Shovel Ears stood up to be married. They crossed their fingers. They told each other other they would remember their promises.

Pig Wisps

And Pig Wisps had two ropes of pearls twisted down her back and a sweet young face saying, "Here we come—where from?"

Kiss Me

Many years ago when pigs climbed chimneys and chased cats up into the trees, away back, so they say, there was a lumber king who lived in a river city with many wildcats in the timbers near by.

And the lumber king said, "I am losing my hair and my teeth and I am tired of many things; my only joy is a daughter who is a dancing shaft of light on the ax handles of morning."

She was quick and wild, the lumber king's daughter. She had never kissed. Not her mother nor father nor any sweetheart ever had

a love print from her lips.   Proud she was.
They called her Kiss Me.

She didn't like that name, Kiss Me.   They
never called her that when she was listening.
If she happened to be listening they called her
Find Me, Lose Me, Get Me.   They never
mentioned kisses because they knew she would
run away and be what her father called her,
"a dancing shaft of light on the ax handles
of morning."

But—when she was not listening they asked,
"Where is Kiss Me to-day?"   Or they would
say, "Every morning Kiss Me gets more beautiful—I wonder if she will ever in her young
life get a kiss from a man good enough to
kiss her."

One day Kiss Me was lost.   She went out
on a horse with a gun to hunt wildcats in the
timbers near by.   Since the day before, she
was gone.   All night she was out in a snowstorm with a horse and a gun hunting wild-

Out into the snowstorm Flax Eyes rode that day

cats. And the storm of the blowing snow was coming worse on the second day.

It was then the lumber king called in a long, loose, young man with a leather face and hay in his hair. And the king said, "Flax Eyes, you are the laziest careless man in the river lumber country—go out in the snowstorm now, among the wildcats, where Kiss Me is fighting for her life—and save her."

"I am the hero. I am the man who knows how. I am the man who has been waiting for this chance," said Flax Eyes.

On a horse, with a gun, out into the snowstorm Flax Eyes rode that day. Far, far away he rode to where Kiss Me, the quick wild Kiss Me, was standing with her back against a big rock fighting off the wildcats.

In that country the snowstorms make the wildcats wilder—and Kiss Me was tired of shooting wildcats, tired of fighting in the snow, nearly ready to give up and let the wildcats have her.

Then Flax Eyes came. The wildcats jumped at him, and he threw them off. More wildcats came, jumping straight at his face. He took hold of those wildcats by the necks and threw them over the big rock, up into the trees, away into the snow and the wind.

At last he took all the wildcats one by one and threw them so far they couldn't come back. He put Kiss Me on her horse, rode back to the lumber king and said lazy and careless, "This is us."

The lumber king saw the face of Flax Eyes was all covered with cross marks like the letter X. And the lumber king saw the wildcats had torn the shirt off Flax Eyes and on the skin of his chest, shoulders, arms, were the cross marks of the wildcats' claws, cross marks like the letter X.

So the king went to the men who change the alphabets and they put the cross marks of the wildcats' claws, for a new letter, the letter

Kiss Me

X, near the end of the alphabet. And at the
wedding of Kiss Me and Flax Eyes, the men
who change the alphabets came with wildcat
claws crossed like the letter X.

Blue Silver

Long ago when the years were dark and the black rains used to come with strong winds and blow the front porches off houses, and pick chimneys off houses, and blow them onto other houses, long ago when people had understanding about rain and wind, there was a rich man with a daughter he loved better than anything else in the world.

And one night when the black rain came with a strong wind blowing off front porches and picking off chimneys, the daughter of the rich man fell asleep into a deep sleep.

In the morning they couldn't wake her.

Blue Silver

The black rain with the strong wind kept up all that day while she kept on sleeping in a deep sleep.

Men and women with music and flowers came in, boys and girls, her playmates, came in—singing songs and calling her name. And she went on sleeping.

All the time her arms were crossed on her breast, the left arm crossing the right arm like a letter X.

Two days more, five days, six, seven days went by—and all the time the black rain with a strong wind blowing—and the daughter of the rich man never woke up to listen to the music nor to smell the flowers nor to hear her playmates singing songs and calling her name.

She stayed sleeping in a deep sleep—with her arms crossed on her breast—the left arm crossing the right arm like a letter X.

So they made a long silver box, just long enough to reach from her head to her feet.

And they put on her a blue silver dress and

a blue silver band around her forehead and blue silver shoes on her feet.

There were soft blue silk and silver sleeves to cover her left arm and her right arm—the two arms crossed on her breast like the letter X.

They took the silver box and carried it to a corner of the garden where she used to go to look at blue lilacs and climbing blue morning glories in patches of silver lights.

Among the old leaves of blue lilacs and morning glories they dug a place for the silver box to be laid in.

And men and women with music and flowers stood by the silver box, and her old playmates, singing songs she used to sing—and calling her name.

When it was all over and they all went away they remembered one thing most of all.

And that was her arms in the soft silk and blue silver sleeves, the left arm crossing over the right arm like the letter X.

Somebody went to the king of the country and told him how it all happened, how the black rains with a strong wind came, the deep sleep, the singing playmates, the silver box—and the soft silk and blue silver sleeves on the left arm crossing the right arm like the letter X.

Before that there never was a letter X in the alphabet. It was then the king said, "We shall put the crossed arms in the alphabet; we shall have a new letter called X, so everybody will understand a funeral is beautiful if there are young singing playmates."